ArtScroll® Youth Series

Rabbi Nosson Scherman / Rabbi Gedaliah Zlotowitz
General Editors
Rabbi Meir Zlotowitz ז״ל, *Founder*

1

The Starlight Sisters

Published by

ARTSCROLL®
Mesorah Publications, ltd

Ora's Story: SECOND FIDDLE

Libby Lazewnik

FIRST EDITION
First Impression … August 2023

Published and Distributed by
MESORAH PUBLICATIONS, LTD.
313 Regina Avenue / Rahway, N.J 07065

Distributed in Europe by
LEHMANNS
Unit E, Viking Business Park
Rolling Mill Road
Jarow, Tyne & Wear, NE32 3DP
England

Distributed in Australia and New Zealand by
GOLDS WORLDS OF JUDAICA
3-13 William Street
Balaclava, Melbourne 3183
Victoria, Australia

Distributed in Israel by
SIFRIATI / A. GITLER — BOOKS
POB 2351
Bnei Brak 51122

Distributed in South Africa by
KOLLEL BOOKSHOP
Northfield Centre, 17 Northfield Avenue
Glenhazel 2192, Johannesburg, South Africa

ARTSCROLL® YOUTH SERIES
THE STARLIGHT SISTERS — VOLUME 1
ORA'S STORY: SECOND FIDDLE
© *Copyright 2023, by* MESORAH PUBLICATIONS, Ltd.
313 Regina Avenue / Rahway, N.J. 07065 / (718) 921-9000 / www.artscroll.com

---

ISBN 10: 1-4226-3348-9
ISBN 13: 978-1-4226-3348-9

Typography by CompuScribe at ArtScroll Studios, Ltd.

Printed in PRC

For my dear granddaughter

Shoshana Wainhaus

Beautiful middos
An amazing imagination
And you love to read.
What could be better?

Table of Contents

Chapter 1: Introducing Ora   9

Chapter 2: Wide Awake at Midnight   15

Chapter 3: Something New   21

Chapter 4: Something Huge   25

Chapter 5: Two Worlds   31

Chapter 6: The Audition   37

Chapter 7: Waiting   44

Chapter 8: Daydreams   48

Chapter 9: New Beginnings   55

Chapter 10: Starlight   60

Chapter 11: First Impressions   66

Chapter 12: One Tiny Mosquito   73

Chapter 13: Sooo Special   78

Chapter 14: Out in the Cold   84

Chapter 15: Problems   90

Chapter 16: More Problems   93

Chapter 17: A Cut Above   97

Chapter 18: The Apology   102

Chapter 19: Three's a Crowd   108

Chapter 20: The Thundercloud   114
Chapter 21: Binny in Trouble   121
Chapter 22: Ora to the Rescue   128
Chapter 23: Ora Is Gracious   134
Chapter 24: Chol HaMoed Blues   141
Chapter 25: Back to School   148
Chapter 26: Strike Two   154
Chapter 27: A Team Player   160
Chapter 28: Triple Whammy   166
Chapter 29: All Up to Ora   170
Chapter 30: Going It Alone   175
Chapter 31: Talks and Thrills   179
Chapter 32: Missing Ora   184
Chapter 33: Useless Efforts   189
Chapter 34: Where's the Happiness?   194
Chapter 35: A New Resolution   199
Chapter 36: A Strange Encounter   205
Chapter 37: Excitement in the Air   211
Chapter 38: A Mystery   216
Chapter 39: The Decision   220
Chapter 40: Pile on the Rewards!   225
Chapter 41: Prep and Prayer   231
Chapter 42: Slamming Doors   235
Chapter 43: Plans for Binny   241
Chapter 44: A Better Future   247
Chapter 45: Work... or Fun?   253
Chapter 46: The Pact   257
Chapter 47: The Performance   262
Chapter 48: Only the Beginning   268

Chapter 1

Introducing Ora

My name is Ora M. Weiss. The "M" stands for Miriam, though my mother sometimes says that it stands for "Moody."

The reason for that is simple. My mother calls me moody because I *am*. Sometimes I can feel six different things almost before I get out of bed! Take this morning, for example.

I woke up to find sunshine streaming through my window. That made me happy. The splotches of sunlight on the wall and across my blanket made me dizzy with delight. It made me feel that it was going to be a good day. Maybe even a fabulous day! I turned over, smiling... And then I saw my sister Bassi brushing her hair in front of the mirror.

I'm talking about my *perfect* sister Bassi. The one with the perfect hair to match her perfect face and perfect personality.

Seeing in the mirror that I was awake, my perfectly beautiful big sister said, "Oh, good. I was just going to wake you, Ora. It's getting late."

She didn't say it in a bossy way, like the kind of big sister who always thinks she knows better than you. She said it as if it really mattered to her that I be on time for school. My perfect, beautiful, *caring* big sister.

I could never be like Bassi. I could never be half as pretty, or half as kind. Suddenly, as I thought these things, my mood took a nosedive. That's the way it goes, see? Happy one minute, down in the dumps the next.

Can you blame my mother for saying that "Moody" is my middle name?

I don't know why I should have felt grumpy just because my sister was sitting there, brushing her hair and smiling her sunny smile — but I did. Maybe it was because it reminded me of all the many ways that Bassi outshines me. It's hard to always feel second-best.

After my sister left the room, I started getting ready for school and gradually cheered up. There's something about seeing crisp piles of neatly folded clothing in my dresser drawers, with everything exactly where it belongs, that always lifts my spirits. Little things can do that sometimes. Add that to the sunshine streaming through the window, and pretty soon I was smiling again. But for how long?

My father always tells me that I have to learn to master my moods, and not let them master *me*. I know that Abba's right… but *knowing* it and *doing* it are two different things. I would love to be less moody — but so far, I haven't found the trick to making that happen.

Still, as I got ready for school, I decided to try. I resolved to be of good cheer for the rest of the day.

My resolution didn't last long.

When I went downstairs for breakfast, the rest of the family, except for my father, were already in the kitchen. Mommy was busy preparing breakfast, and everyone else was busy eating it. I said, "No, thank you" to my mother's offer of scrambled eggs, and was just starting to pour myself a bowl of cereal when I heard Bassi say, "Ma, can I bring my friends home after school today? We want to study for our Chumash test together."

Did I mention that my perfect big sister also has a zillion friends?

Hearing her ask that question, I instantly saw red. Gone was my resolution to be cheerful. Gone was everything except the way I felt at that second.

"*Again*?" I screeched.

My sister turned to me in surprise. "What's the problem?"

"The problem," I said, trying to speak below a yell and not succeeding very well, "is simple. If you and your friends will be using our room, what am *I* supposed to do?"

It was my mother who answered.

"You'll have the rest of the house, Ora," she said calmly. "Please don't be difficult." To Bassi, she said, "Of course your friends can come. There are some brownies in the freezer if you want to serve them a treat."

That's the way it goes in my house. Bassi gets the brownies, and I get "Please don't be difficult, Ora."

I rolled my eyes and gave a disgruntled sort of grunt.

But if I expected sympathy, I was disappointed. Mommy just went on scrambling eggs. Bassi continued wrapping up her sandwich for lunch. My brother Binny snickered at my eye roll, and little Huvi giggled just because Binny did. The only one who didn't laugh at me was baby Shmulie, because he was too young to get the joke.

"Ora's being a sourpuss," Huvi announced, when she'd finished giggling.

"So what else is new?" asked Binny.

I glared at Binny. I wished that my siblings would quit providing a running commentary on my moods.

Then again, who could blame them? My ups and downs were pretty good entertainment.

If it weren't for one thing, I would be absolutely convinced that my life is miserable. That everyone else — especially my big sister — got all the gifts to make them special, while I got nothing.

The reason I *don't* feel that way — at least, not all the time — is because I do have one gift. One fabulous gift that actually makes me very happy.

I'm talking about my voice.

Bassi may be just about perfect in every way that counts, but I can sing rings around her.

It's too bad that I don't get to use my singing voice that much. Mostly just on Shabbos, when I sing *zemiros* with my family, and in camp in the summer. Last year, in fifth grade, our class made a modest choir and invited our mothers to come. I was the soloist. That was the highlight of my life so far.

But you can be sure I wasn't singing as I made my way to school that morning. I was scuffing my feet on the sidewalk and glowering at the unfairness of it all. The day was unusually hot for early May, with pretty pink or white buds popping out on all the trees I passed. I enjoyed the buds, but I was *not* looking forward to coming home after school to find the house filled with Bassi's friends.

If you think I was overreacting, that's because you don't know the whole picture. The reason it hurt so much was because… to tell you the truth, I was having some trouble in the friends department myself. And had been all year.

When my best friend since kindergarten moved away with her family last summer, I was devastated. I would have felt even worse if I'd known how hard it would be to find someone to fill the void. Gila and I had been together, in school and camp, for practically as long as I could remember. She was a built-in companion, twelve months a year. After she left, I felt like a boat bobbing along on the ocean with nothing to connect it to the shore. I was unmoored. Off balance.

I was also very out of practice in the friends-making department.

It was after Pesach already — nearly the end of the year — and so far, all I'd done was drift from one group of girls to another. These days I mostly hung around with Lana and Shoshie, though I can't say I enjoyed it much. That's because I was utterly uninterested in most of the things that Lana and Shoshie liked to talk about.

They were into the newest haircuts, and the latest styles, and finding a pair of shoes to match the exact color of their new Shabbos dress. I like being in style as much as the next person, but did we really have to *talk* about it all the time?

So why, you ask, was I hanging around with these girls? I often asked myself that same question. The reason was simple: I needed *someone*. Hanging around all by myself would have made me look nerdy. Even worse, it would have left me feeling lonely. And who wants that?

Not me, that's for sure.

So I kept on hanging around with two classmates whom I didn't really know and who weren't all that interested in knowing me. While all along, deep inside, I was waiting for a *real* friend to come into my life.

I might have to wait a long time... or she might be just around the corner. I had no way of knowing which one it would be. I could only wait. And hope.

I walked to school that morning feeling plenty sorry for myself.

If only I could have peered around the next corner — into the future, I mean — I'd have seen something that would make me start feeling something else entirely.

Something that would turn my grumpy mood right around — in a *huge* way!

Chapter 2

Wide Awake at Midnight

Sometimes, when Lana or Shoshie really got on my nerves, I would wonder if being lonely might not be better.

I would look around at all the girls in my class who had friends they actually liked to spend time with, and I would remember my super-special years with Gila. I would remember how nice it is to be with someone whose company you enjoy. Someone who, when you offer an opinion or tell them an idea, listens to you, and maybe even offers an opinion back... instead of just ignoring you or changing the subject to one they like better.

Somewhere, I knew there was a person who could be my new best friend. So far, though, I hadn't found her. But that didn't mean I wouldn't keep on looking...

"What took you so long?" Lana asked, as I rushed up

to join them outside the school building at the end of the day.

"Sorry —" I huffed, trying to catch my breath. "I had to go back for my notebook."

"Why," Lana complained, as we crossed the street and started the walk home, "can't you *ever* remember things when you're supposed to?"

"Sometimes I do," I defended myself.

"Not often enough. I'm getting tired of waiting for you all the time, Ora."

Well, I was tired, too — tired of Lana's griping. But I bit my tongue. Like I said, I needed companions. And, right now, these two girls were it.

As we walked, they started a fascinating discussion about our English teacher's new *sheitel*. They had noticed (as I had not) that she was wearing a different *sheitel* that day and were eagerly comparing the old one to the new one. I listened politely for a while, and then tuned out. I had nothing to add to the discussion and, to be honest, my own thoughts interested me more.

I thought about how much I loved gorgeous spring days like this, when you can see buds on the trees and splashes of color everywhere. If the freezing winter wind can feel like a sword, the soft spring air is like someone brushing you with a feather. Some of the houses we passed had pretty gardens, and I dawdled so long, looking at them, that Lana finally snapped at me to hurry up and not keep them waiting *again*.

As if she felt bad about Lana's harping, Shoshie asked me how I'd done on our math test that day.

I shrugged. "Okay, I guess." Actually, it was more than

okay. I'm pretty good with numbers, and anyway the test hadn't been too hard.

"*I* thought it was awful," Shoshie said with a shudder. "If I bring home one more bad mark in math, my parents are going to get me a tutor."

"Poor you!" Lana exclaimed.

I said nothing. I didn't think having a tutor was the end of the world, especially if it would make Shoshie more confident in math. But it's no use arguing with Lana. She hates losing an argument and would spend the rest of the walk trying to get me to see things her way. Just thinking about that made me feel bored.

We reached my corner first. I waved good-bye and watched them continue on down the block before heading for my own house. The afternoon was so nice that I didn't want to go indoors yet. The breeze was just right: warm but not hot, and gentle enough so that you enjoyed it without really noticing it. I lingered outside for a while, just soaking it in, and was in a pretty good mood when I finally went inside, even though walking home with Lana and Shoshie usually left me grumpy.

But my upbeat mood flew away the second I set foot in the house and heard girls' voices filling the air. Bassi and her friends! I had forgotten that they would be here when I came home.

I came into the kitchen to find them polishing off a plate of brownies, washed down with glasses of cold milk.

"I don't suppose you left any for me?" I asked sarcastically.

My sister smiled. "Actually, I did. It's in a baggie in the fridge."

That took the wind right out of my sails. It's hard to be mad at someone when they're so *nice*. So I just scowled some more and waited until they all trooped upstairs to do their studying. Then I opened the fridge, took out the brownies and the milk, and had my own lonely snack at the kitchen table.

I was nearly done when my mother walked in. "Hi, Ora. How was your day?"

"Not bad," I said, picking the last brownie crumbs up with my finger. "Except for English class."

"Oh? What happened?"

"My teacher criticized me. She said she doesn't understand why I can't write the way Bassi does. You know — perfect grammar and all."

My mother frowned. She didn't like it when teachers compared me to my sister. As a matter of fact, neither did I. But it happened so often that I was used to it by now. Most of my teachers had taught Bassi, and let's just say that their comparisons did not flatter me.

Mommy wanted to cheer me up. "Everyone is good at different things," she said. "For instance, you get better marks in math and science than Bassi does."

Big deal, I wanted to say. Bassi outdid me at just about everything else, and my teachers never let me forget it.

But I didn't say it, because I knew that Mommy was trying to make me feel better. So I just gave her a half-smile, put the milk back in the fridge, and went into the living room.

I would curl up on the couch and read until Bassi's friends finally went home and I could have my room back.

Usually, I sleep like a log. For some reason, that didn't happen that night.

I read for a long time, waiting for my eyelids to droop. I finished that book and started another one, but I still didn't feel sleepy. Even when I finally turned off the light, I dropped into a light doze and then woke up again an hour later, wide-awake.

Bassi was sound asleep in the other bed. The glowing red numbers on my bedside clock said it was nearly midnight. Around me, the house was quiet. Peaceful. I wished I could just drop back into sleep but didn't think it was going to happen anytime soon. I decided to go downstairs for a drink.

I heard the voices before I reached the kitchen. I know it's not polite to eavesdrop, but there was something about my parents' hushed voices that made me stop outside the door and listen.

"I'm not happy with Ora's attitude toward Bassi," Mommy was saying. "She's always comparing herself to her big sister and feeling as if she can't measure up."

I clenched my fists. It's one thing to know something about yourself — and a whole other thing to hear your own mother say it out loud.

"And," Mommy continued, "as if it's not bad enough at home, the teachers keep comparing her to Bassi, too."

"Not a good situation," my father agreed.

"No, it's not," my mother said in a grim voice. "It seems as if Ora can't even *look* at Bassi without feeling bad."

Abba said something I couldn't quite catch. Then he

added a few more words, almost under his breath. They sounded like, "Attack of the green-eyed monster…"

"So maybe the new school will be the solution," my mother said hopefully. She said it in a way that told me they had already discussed the subject at length. "Especially *this* kind of school."

"Well," Abba said, "it certainly sounds like it's worth a try."

New school?

Solution?

Worth a try?

I stood outside the kitchen door with my mouth hanging open, wondering what they were talking about.

Standing there and listening in the dimness, as the minutes ticked on to midnight, I had no idea that my entire life was about to change — big time!

Chapter 3

Something New

I fell asleep burning with questions. The flames of my curiosity were even hotter when I woke up.

I wanted desperately to ask my mother what she and Abba had been talking about the night before but was embarrassed to admit that I'd been eavesdropping. So I forced myself to smile and say good morning to Mommy as if I'd heard nothing at all.

My father sometimes comes home from Shacharis before he goes to work, and that's what he did that morning. He sat down to have breakfast with us. About halfway through, he remembered something.

"Binny," he told my brother, "I met Mr. Grossbaum in shul this morning."

"Who?" Binny asked. He was busy trying to figure out the puzzle on the back of the cereal box and was not really listening.

"Pay attention, please," Abba said. "Mr. Grossbaum?

Our neighbor?"

"Oh, right. Him." Mr. Grossbaum was not a favorite of the kids on our block. He was always scolding them for making too much noise and for letting their balls land on his property.

"Yes, him," Abba said. "He doesn't like you boys tramping through his back yard. He says it damages his landscaping."

Binny scowled. "But *all* the kids use the back yards to get to each other's houses. It's much faster that way!"

"I know. But Mr. Grossbaum doesn't like it, and you need to respect his wishes."

My brother was not happy about this, but he knew better than to argue. Besides, what was the point? It wasn't our father who was taking away the kids' shortcut. It was Mr. Grossbaum.

So Binny just nodded his head and went back to his puzzle.

My baby brother Shmulie decided that this would be a good time to toss his bowl of oatmeal off his highchair tray. Then, for good measure, he threw his spoon, too. He leaned over the side of the highchair to see where it had landed. Not finding it anywhere, he began making the squealing sounds that meant he was about to start crying.

We all found out where it was a second later. "Mommy!" Huvi wailed. "Shmulie threw his spoon at me!"

I looked over at my little sister. The oatmeal-encrusted spoon was stuck in her hair like some kind of weird new barrette. *Eeew.*

"He didn't mean to throw it at you, sweetie," Mommy

said, plucking out the dirty spoon and tossing it in the sink before Huvi could start crying, too. "Come on, let's get that gunk out of your hair."

My mother gave Shmulie another spoon and led Huvi to the bathroom to clean her up. Binny was still doing his puzzle and Bassi stood up to pack her bag for school. Here was my chance.

"So," I said brightly to my father. "What's new?"

I held my breath, hoping he'd say something about what he and Mommy had been discussing the night before. But he just smiled, and said, "Oh, this and that. How about you?"

I had nothing new to report. Bassi said something about having a gazillion tests to study for before the year ended.

"Yeah, but when the tests are over, you'll graduate eighth grade," I told her. "You'll finally be finished with elementary school."

"Big deal," Binny piped up, tearing his eyes away from his cereal box. "She'll just have to start all over again in high school next year."

"I happen to *like* the school I'm in," Bassi said. "I'm not in a rush to leave."

Again, in my mind, I heard my parents' hushed voices... talking about a possible solution for me. "*Especially* this *kind of school*," Mommy had said.

What kind of school? And why would it be good for me?

I was forced to leave the house with none of my questions answered. But just having the mystery in the back of my mind made the day feel different.

Any time I felt bored, or annoyed about something, I would remember my parents' mysterious words and feel a flutter of excitement instead. When Lana said something snippy, I didn't mind as much. Even when I realized that I'd forgotten to pack my favorite snack for recess, I hardly cared.

Something new was getting ready to happen. It was lurking right around the corner — out of sight but not far away. I could feel it in my bones.

I just wished I knew exactly what it was. If my parents didn't tell me soon, I felt as if I'd explode with curiosity!

Luckily for me, I didn't have to wait much longer.

Chapter 4
Something Huge

I had actually forgotten all about the overheard conversation and was curled up on the couch with a book that evening, yawning my head off and thinking about having an early bedtime to make up for not getting much sleep the night before, when my mother poked her head into the living room. "Ora? Can you come in here a minute?"

The house was peaceful. Bassi was in our room, finishing up some homework. Binny was in *his* room, doing whatever it is he likes to do before bedtime. Reading an adventure book, maybe, or building something with his Lego. Sometimes he kicks around a soccer ball, forgetting that my mother doesn't like it. Huvi and Shmulie had been tucked in hours ago. I trailed my mother into the kitchen, thinking about maybe having a cookie before I went to bed.

Then, to my surprise, I saw that the kitchen wasn't

empty. Abba was there. He was sitting at the table as though he'd been waiting for me.

I looked at his face, and then at Mommy's, and my heart gave an odd little bump. As if it were sitting up and shouting, *"Red Alert! Red Alert! Something's happening! Something HUGE!"*

One thing, for sure, I wasn't the tiniest bit sleepy anymore.

"Have a seat," Abba invited.

I slid into a chair opposite him. My mother took a third one, turning the three of us into a triangle. A solemn triangle in the heart of the quiet house.

"So, we've been thinking," Mommy began.

Now that my heart had jolted awake, it was pounding harder than usual. I clenched my fists, my nails digging into my palms, as I waited to hear what she and Abba had been thinking about... *and*, I assumed, what they'd also been talking about the night before.

"You don't seem so happy in school this year," Mommy said. "Since Gila moved away."

"I'm not," I said quickly.

"You don't seem to have found any good friends to replace her."

I shook my head. "I wish."

"And I don't like the way your teachers keep comparing you to your older sister." She gave me a sad look. "Or the way *you're* always comparing yourself to her."

Mommy didn't seem to expect an answer, so I kept quiet and kept listening. It was my father who spoke next.

"It's no fun to always feel like you have to play second fiddle to someone else," Abba said thoughtfully

I didn't understand. "Second fiddle?" I asked.

"Think about a band. It has different instruments, right? Well, suppose someone's job is to play the fiddle in the band. He's really good at it, too. And then suppose they hire a *second* musician to also play the fiddle. But he's not the star of the show. He's just there to back up the first performer. He's always sort of in the shade, because he's just the 'second fiddle.'"

I thought about me and Bassi, and I nodded. "You're right. I don't like being second fiddle all the time. I want to be *first* fiddle!"

My parents smiled.

"That's kind of what we thought. So, we were wondering," Abba continued, "if this wouldn't be the right time for... a change."

I looked from my father's face to my mother's face, and then back again. "Ch-change?" Now that it was coming, I was not so sure I wanted to hear.

"There's a new school opening up this fall," Mommy said. "It's going to be a Bais Yaakov school — but with a special twist."

"Something," Abba added, "that may be right up your alley."

I could hear a faint thumping from upstairs, which probably meant that Binny was practicing his soccer moves even though Mommy had told him a thousand times to only play ball outside. Even more faintly, I could hear Bassi's voice on the phone with one of her friends. The kitchen felt like an island, far away from everyone and everything else.

"What do you mean?" I asked. "What alley?"

My parents exchanged a look. It was Mommy who started talking again.

"The new school is going to be a little different," she said. "You know how *chesed* organizations are always having dinners and lunches, banquets and Chinese auctions and things like that, to raise money for *tzedakah*?"

I nodded.

"Well, many of those organizations would *love* to have some top-notch entertainment at their events — to make their guests happy and encourage them to donate generously to the cause. And, for an all-women event, they would naturally want all-girl entertainment."

"What kind of entertainment?"

"You know. A choir. Or a dance group. Things like that."

My heart, which had settled down a bit, started pounding wildly again. I repeated the magic word. "Choir?"

"Yes," said Abba. "This new school will be a regular Bais Yaakov, but it will also train *frum* girls to be top-notch performers, ready to put on a first-rate performance for any women's organization that wants them to provide entertainment at their events."

"The organizations would pay the school to have the girls perform," Mommy added. "That way, both the *tzedakah* organizations and the school would benefit."

Abba leaned toward me, his eyes alive with excitement. "It's a really original idea, Ora. Apart from the usual school curriculum, they're going to have professional instructors to train the girls' voices and teach them music, dance, and so on!"

I was so excited that it was hard to breathe. "And I...
I...?"

"If you're interested," Mommy said, "we thought you
might want to audition for the school."

I stared at her. "Audition?"

"Yes. You'd have to be interviewed by the principal
first, to see if you're a good candidate — just like in
any other school. But they'll also want to hear you sing.
They're only going to accept girls who can sing, dance, or
play an instrument very well."

"But I thought you said they're planning to give lessons."

"They are. But they're looking for girls who have some
solid talent to work with," Abba told me. "Like I said —
they want to produce top-notch performers."

I tried to think about this, but my head was swimming.
"Do you really think they'd accept me? I don't have professional training or anything. I just like to sing."

"You have a lovely voice," my mother said. "The school
would provide the training... *if* they decide to accept you
as a student."

"If," I echoed hollowly. Some of my excitement faded,
and fear crept in to take its place.

My father looked me straight in the eye. "It would be
a big commitment, Ora. You'd have a longer school day
than usual, because you'd be training and rehearsing on
top of your regular classes."

"*And* you'd have to commit to keeping up with your
schoolwork," my mother said.

"And all that is on top of the drive," Abba put in. "The
school will be located in Valley Stream, in the vicinity

of North Woodmere. That's over 45 minutes from here. Each way."

I didn't care if it was a hundred miles away. I didn't care about anything. Let them pile on the schoolwork, the homework — anything! If I was in a place where I could sing, I'd be happy. I *knew* I would.

"I want to go," I said.

My parents exchanged another look. Then Abba said, "Take some time to think it over, Ora. This would be a big change for you."

"And, like Abba said, a big commitment," Mommy added.

There was only one thing I could say to that, so I said it. Again.

"I want to go."

If I'd thought it was hard to fall asleep the night before, that was nothing compared to the way I felt after that talk with my parents.

Something new was happening. Something *huge*!

After this whole, miserable slog of a year, I was finally going to have a chance to start over somewhere else. Somewhere fresh. Somewhere different. Somewhere exciting!

Of course, I'd have to get through an interview and an audition first. There was no guarantee that they'd accept me. Still, it was a chance. A chance that I intended to grab with both hands.

When I finally did fall asleep, it was with a huge smile on my face.

Chapter 5

Two Worlds

For the next week, I lived in two different worlds.

The first world was the one I'd been living in until yesterday. Wake up in the morning, gulp down some breakfast, go to school. Deal with classes and teachers. Walk home with Lana and Shoshie, feeling bored and restless and wishing, wishing, wishing for a real friend.

Then do my homework, read a book, and crawl into bed... so I could fall asleep and do it all over again the next day.

But the second world — oh, how different that one was! So far, it existed only in my imagination. But it felt as real as could be.

In that world, I was in a different place. One that would not only teach me the usual things that everyone learns in school but would also train my voice and let me sing!

In that world, I would open my eyes each morning and literally jump out of bed, eager for the new day to begin.

In that world, there would be the usual lessons and homework and tests — but there would also be choirs and rehearsals and exciting performances!

It was hard to keep the two worlds from colliding with each other.

How could I concentrate in class, when all I wanted to do was sit and wonder if I'd be accepted into the new school? My mother had called the people in charge on the morning after our talk, and they gave me an appointment for an interview and an audition. The appointment was a whole week away. How in the world was I supposed to survive till then?

At the same time, I was dreading it so much that a horde of butterflies started doing a peculiar dance in the pit of my stomach. I tried my best to ignore them, but I could tell that they wouldn't be going anywhere until my audition was over.

Lana is pretty smart. She soon guessed that something was up.

"What's going on with you?" she demanded crossly, when she'd asked me the same question three times and I just kept giving her a blank stare and saying, "What?"

"Nothing. I'm fine." We were walking home from school as usual.

"Well, you're not *acting* fine. You're acting weird."

"Sorry." I tried to sweeten my answer with a smile.

Even my smile must have looked suspicious, because she gave me an annoyed look and then turned to Shoshie. "Ora *is* acting weird, right?"

Shoshie shrugged. "She seems the same as usual to me."

"Well, not to *me*." Lana tossed her head and stomped ahead of us both. Shoshie and I hurried to keep up. The three of us walked in silence for a while.

I didn't mind the silence. It gave me a chance to listen to the birds that were filling the air with song from their hidden places in the trees. Once, when I was younger, I'd spent a whole summer trying to learn the different sounds that birds make. I could still recognize some of them. But Lana didn't give me much time to enjoy the birdsong. Before long, she was talking again. She was describing an outfit that she'd seen when out shopping with her mother. Shoshie listened raptly. I can't honestly say that I did the same.

My parents had urged me to keep the news about the new school to myself for the time being, so I was doing just that. But it wasn't easy. The new school was all I could think about and all I wanted to talk about.

Thank goodness I didn't have the same problem at home. There, I could talk to my heart's content. And I did!

On the very first night after I heard about the new school, I regaled Bassi, Binny, and little Huvi with information about it.

"It's going to be called the Bais Yaakov of Valley Stream," I told them. "Also, JAPA."

"What does that stand for?" Bassi asked. She was sitting at her desk, the chair turned around to face Huvi and me, both of us perched on my bed, and Binny, sitting crossed-legged on the floor.

"It stands for Jewish Academy for the Performing Arts," I said proudly, as if the name was a badge that I was wearing instead of a school that hadn't even accepted me yet. "They told Mommy that they're only accepting a small number of girls — no more than ten or twelve in each grade."

"How many grades will the school have altogether?" Binny asked.

"Only three, at first — seventh, eighth, and ninth. Eventually they want to have a whole high school, but they're starting small."

"Lucky for you that you'll be in seventh grade next year," Binny remarked.

Yes, lucky me!

Then my happiness died away, and the butterflies came back.

"*If* I get accepted," I reminded him. "They're probably interviewing tons of girls." I sighed dreamily. "Can you imagine? Being in a choir and getting to sing every single day..."

Huvi's lower lip started trembling. "*I* want to go to a singing school, too!"

My little sister is a very emotional person. When she's happy, she's on top of the world. But when something makes her sad, she can weep and wail as if her heart is breaking. She looked that way now.

Binny took one look at Huvi, clapped his hands over his ears, and ran out of the room, yelling, "Look out! Hurricane warning!" I could hear him laughing all the way down the hall to his own room.

I looked uneasily at Huvi, whose eyes were rapidly filling with tears. But Bassi acted fast. Scooping the four-year-old into her arms, she hugged her tight and said, "You and me are going to have a singing school of our own — right here at home!"

Huvi squirmed around to look up at her. "Really?"

"Really. Ready for our first class?"

My little sister nodded excitedly. The tears were gone.

"The itsy-bitsy spider climbed up the water spout," Bassi sang. Pretty soon, Huvi was singing along in her high, thin voice. When the song was done, Huvi begged for another. Bassi led her in a rousing rendition of "Twinkle, Twinkle, Little Star." Then Huvi hopped off Bassi's knee to go tell Mommy that *she* was in a singing school, too! We watched her go with a smile.

"There's something I don't get," Bassi said, when we were alone. "It's near the end of May already. I registered for high school months ago. Why is the new school still interviewing students so late in the year?"

"Mommy explained that to me, too," I said. "Mrs. Mammon — she's the one founding the school and will be the principal — actually planned to open next year. But when people heard about it, they put pressure on her to start the school this coming year. So, she agreed. But, like I said, they're keeping it small for now."

"When's your audition?" my sister wanted to know.

"Next week. Tuesday." Those butterflies were kicking up a real storm now. Thinking about the interview, and especially the audition, made me feel queasy.

"Good luck," Bassi said softly. "I mean that."

I knew she did. Bassi might make *me* green with envy, but she didn't seem to have a jealous bone in her body. I nodded and said, "Thanks."

And just like that, my mood flipped right over again. I forgot all about the audition. I stopped feeling scared and was flying high.

My sister might be perfect — but *she* wasn't the one about to try out for a fabulous new school for the performing arts.

That was *me*. Second-fiddle Ora.

With a chance — just a chance — of turning my whole life around next Tuesday!

Chapter 6

The Audition

"**H**urry, Ora, or we'll be late!"

My mother's voice floated up the stairs. I'd woken up early and been running right on time until I opened my closet to get dressed for my interview. That was when I realized that I didn't have a clue about what to wear.

My school uniform? A weekday dress? A Shabbos dress? Help!

Mommy finally came up to see what was keeping me so long. She gaped at the piles of clothes strewn all over my bed. "What's going on?"

"I don't know what to wear," I moaned.

"Wear anything. It doesn't matter. We don't want to be late for the interview!" My mother sounded as nervous as I felt. She picked up a skirt and top and almost threw them at me. "Hurry!" she urged. She left the room so I could change.

With that decision out of the way, I was ready in no time. A last look in the mirror, a last tug on my curly dark ponytail, a last smile at my reflection in the mirror as I whispered, "Good luck!" — and I was out the door.

The drive to Valley Stream was long and short at the same time. When we got caught in a traffic jam and all I could see was a river of cars ahead of us, all waiting for a chance to move forward a few inches, I jiggled in my seat as though doing that could make the car go faster. This was one time I didn't want to be late!

When the traffic cleared up and we were moving again, I sat back and tried to relax. Then I heard my mother say, "We're nearly there, Ora. About five minutes." My stomach clenched so tightly that I literally lost my breath. I felt as if someone had punched me in the solar plexus. I wished I was anywhere but where I was. I wished the drive could be longer — say, about a few weeks longer…

"This is it," Mommy said. I looked out the window to where she was pointing.

The new school had taken over a building that a different school had used before closing down last year.

The place was small but charming, with big glass windows in front and a lawn stretching like an emerald sea to the sidewalk on one side and a parking lot on the other. This part of Long Island was much more spread out than I was used to in Brooklyn. I followed my mother through a glass door and into the lobby, which led directly to the school office. The scent of fresh paint tickled my nose.

"Please take a seat," a secretary told us in the outer office. "Mrs. Mammon will be with you shortly."

I sat at the very edge of the chair next to my mother, stiff as a board.

"Relax," Mommy whispered, smiling. "We're here, and we're on time. The worst is behind us."

I shook my head. The worst was not behind *me*. I still had to be interviewed by Mrs. Mammon, the principal, and then get through my audition. I closed my eyes and thought, "Please, Hashem, help me get this right. Don't let me mess up!"

When I opened them, my mother was getting to her feet and the secretary was holding open the door to an inner office. "Right this way, please."

It was time.

I liked the way Mrs. Mammon looked. I'm not talking about her clothes or her *sheitel*. I hardly even noticed those things. It was her eyes that captured my attention right from the start. They were smart eyes. They were also kind.

They were eyes that seemed to look right *into* me, as if she could see all the good and the bad that was Ora M. Weiss and was prepared to like me anyway.

The principal asked a lot of questions, but she asked them so calmly that I felt calm as I answered them, too. Sometimes she addressed something to my mother, but mostly she focused on me.

Then she stopped asking questions and started talking to both of us. She told us about what she called the school's "mission statement."

"We are going to be a regular Bais Yaakov in every way," Mrs. Mammon said. "We are going to hold our girls to the highest standards in terms of *middos* and schoolwork. At the same time, our performing arts division will add plenty of excitement. There will be musical training, rehearsals, and performances. That means a lot of hard work. There will be some traveling, too. We need to know that our students will be able to handle it all."

"Oh, I can handle it," I said eagerly. "I'm sure I can!"

Mrs. Mammon smiled and sat back in her big swivel chair. "Thank you very much for coming, both of you." She looked at me. "It's time for your audition now, Ora."

The butterflies were back, an army of them tramping through my insides as the school secretary met us at the door and pointed to a room at the end of the hall. Mommy asked, "Do you want me to come in with you, Ora?"

I nodded my head. The butterflies moved up from my stomach and filled my throat. I couldn't say a word.

We walked in silence down the hall to the door that the secretary had shown us. My mother knocked.

"Come in!" someone called out from inside the room. Mommy opened the door, and I followed her in. A woman was there, younger than Mrs. Mammon, with dark-blond hair and big, square glasses.

"Hi!" she greeted us with a friendly smile. "I'm Miss Sperling. I'm going to be in charge of the choir here. And your name is…?"

"Ora," I croaked. I cleared my throat and tried again. "Ora Weiss."

"Nice to meet you, Ora." She went to sit down at the

piano that was arranged along one wall. "Ready to sing something for me?"

I *wanted* to be ready, but my voice thought otherwise. It simply refused to cooperate.

I felt tight and choked-up inside, as if my throat had turned into a piece of dried-out orange peel. Both Miss Sperling and my mother were looking at me expectantly, but I could barely even talk, let alone sing.

"Would it be easier if your mother left the room?" Miss Sperling asked gently.

I shook my head. Mommy wasn't the problem. It was those stupid butterflies that wouldn't leave me alone.

"She's not usually like this," my mother told Miss Sperling, as if she felt the need to apologize. I felt my cheeks flaming.

"It's okay," Miss Sperling said. "It happens. Ora, can you look at me, please?"

I lifted my eyes to her face. She looked nice. Not threatening at all.

"How about picturing yourself in your room at home. Do you like to sing there?"

I couldn't help smiling, because I was *always* singing in my room. I nodded eagerly.

"Okay, then," Miss Sperling said. "Imagine that you're right there, all by yourself, singing a song that you love."

Picturing myself in my room, among my familiar things — my bed, my books, even the messy pile of clothes I'd left behind when I got ready to come here — made me start to relax. I would just pretend that I was singing in front of my own bedroom mirror. My confidence started flowing back. I could do this!

I looked at Miss Sperling and gave her the name of a song. One of my favorites.

"Great!" Miss Sperling said enthusiastically. She put her hands on the piano's keyboard. "Anytime you're ready…"

As she hit the first note, my voice suddenly freed itself from those butterflies. It launched itself into the air like a bird bursting out of a bush — and began to soar!

I sang as if I were all by myself at home, with nobody listening and nobody judging. I forgot my nervousness and let myself enjoy the words and the music. I could hear the way my voice filled that small room and then started searching for more space. The melody rose and fell, swooped and soared.

It was a great song, and I gave it everything I had. I stood there and sang my heart out.

When the last note died away, I bobbed my head shyly, as if to say, "That's all."

There was a split second of silence. Then Miss Sperling dropped her hands to her lap and took a breath.

"Nice," she said.

"Powerful voice," she added, looking at my mother.

Mommy nodded back, eyes shining.

After that, Miss Sperling sang a few lines of a song I'd never heard before and asked me to sing it back to her. She wanted to see how quickly I could pick up a new melody. I have a good ear and I managed to learn the tune pretty fast. By the time we were done, both Mommy and Miss Sperling were smiling.

And then we were saying good-bye and leaving the charming little building the same way we'd come.

We found our car in the parking lot, where I collapsed into the passenger seat feeling as if I'd just taken off the heaviest backpack in the world.

The audition was behind me. I could breathe again.

Now all that was left was the waiting.

Chapter 7

Waiting

"So, how did it go?" Bassi asked eagerly.

I shrugged. "I thought it went pretty well. But I have no idea what *they* thought. And it's their opinion that counts."

She couldn't argue with me there. "Tell me all about it," she said instead.

So I told my sister about the charming little building with the big lawn out front, and Mrs. Mammon with the kind eyes, and the questions she'd asked me. Then I described Miss Sperling and the audition where I'd almost chickened out, before I managed to sing by pretending that I was safe at home.

Bassi was puzzled. "You're not usually shy about singing in front of other people," she said. "Why was it so hard this time?"

I stared at her in disbelief. Didn't she get how *important* this was to me? How devastated I'd be if I didn't get into the school?

Before my parents had told me about the possible change, I'd been ready to keep on slogging along where I was. But things were different now. Now, I had something to hope for.

But Bassi *didn't* get it. I could see that on her face. She didn't get it because she didn't know about the kind of year I'd just had in the school I was in. Or the kind of dread I'd felt at the thought of messing up in front of Miss Sperling. Bassi didn't have to hope for anything. She already had it all.

So I just lifted my chin and said, "You wouldn't understand."

My sister's face fell, which made me feel bad. I wanted to apologize — but I also didn't want to.

You have everything, Bassi, I thought. *I just want a place where I can shine, too. Is that so terrible?*

"Anyway," I said out loud, partly to make her feel better and partly to make me feel better, "it's nice of you to be interested."

"Of course I'm interested! You're my sister!"

That made me feel bad all over again. I didn't know what else to say, so I made an excuse and left. The living room was empty when I came downstairs. I sat on the couch, closed my eyes, and said a little private *tefillah*.

"Hashem, I know I'm not such a nice person sometimes — especially when it comes to Bassi. But I promise to try harder. Just let me get into the new school, and I'll work my head off to be the best person I can be!"

When I opened my eyes, I felt a little better. Cleaner.

Then I remembered that it might be a long time before

I had an answer from Mrs. Mammon. She had promised to let us know by the end of the school year — meaning, near the end of June. She thought it only right that we be able to go into the summer knowing where we stood.

I sighed. We were still in the month of May.

It was going to be a very long few weeks.

It's one thing to promise that you'll start being a better person, and another thing to actually make it happen. I found that out about two weeks later, at Bassi's eighth-grade graduation.

I went there readily enough, sitting next to my mother prepared to clap like mad whenever my sister's name was mentioned. But that was before I heard them start heaping on the praise. Not surprisingly, she won the graduating class's *middos* award.

She stood there with her big, beautiful smile, happy and modest, as everyone around me applauded with enthusiasm. That should have made me feel even prouder of my sister. Instead — as usual — I was jealous.

That green-eyed monster just wouldn't leave me be.

I knew that when *I* stood at my eighth-grade graduation in a couple of years, nobody would be fawning over me. And I knew the reason why.

Bassi was a first-rate student because she cared enough to want to be one. She was a super-nice person because she worked hard to have fantastic *middos*. Yours truly couldn't say the same about either of those things.

So I sat there, hunched in my seat and pretending to

clap for my sister, while inside I was feeling sour and mean.

The only good thing I can say for myself is that, when we were all together again after the ceremony was over, I didn't let Bassi see how I felt. Jealous I might be, but I wanted her to have this perfect night. Because she sure had earned it.

I kept the smile on my face as my parents told her again and again how proud they were of her, and her friends kept running over to hug her. Somehow, I managed to keep my sourness and my envy from peeking through.

Inside, though, I was wondering: Will it ever be *my* turn to shine?

Chapter 8

Daydreams

The days slogged by, long and muggy. Though it was only June, it felt like mid-summer. It was a little cooler in the mornings when I walked to school, but every afternoon we plodded home practically melting in the sweltering sun beating down on our heads.

With camp coming up, all Lana and Shoshie could talk about was — what else? — shopping for clothes.

I trudged along, listening to Lana describe all the cute things she and her mother had bought for camp, and then to Shoshie describe the same things all over again. As I tried my best not to yawn, all I could think about was getting home and having a cold, cold drink.

"What about you?" Lana asked me. "Are you all done with your camp shopping?"

"I guess so," I said with a shrug. "My mother is pretty much taking care of it."

"*What*?" she screeched. "You don't even go shopping

with her?"

"Not unless I can't help it."

"But what if you don't like what she gets? What if it's not the right style?"

I was too hot and tired to even bother thinking of a clever answer. I just shrugged again, and mumbled, "It'll be fine."

Lana gave me a pitying look. I was glad when Shoshie suddenly remembered something she'd forgotten to say before, because it took the attention away from me. By the time Shoshie finished her story, we were at my corner, and I was waving good-bye.

Like I said, the only thing on my mind was that cold drink and relaxing in my air-conditioned room before supper. I pushed open the front door and dumped my backpack on the floor. Mommy doesn't like when we leave our stuff there, but I figured I'd be back to take care of it in a minute or two. After I had that drink.

"I'm home!" I announced, walking into the kitchen. "Is there anything cold to drink in the fridge? I'm so parched, I could — "

That's when I saw my mother's face. It was shining all over, and she was holding something in her hand. Something long and white.

"The letter came today," Mommy said, beaming. "It was addressed to Abba and me, so I opened it." She held it out. "Here."

My heart started making a super-loud racket inside my chest. My hand shook as I reached for the envelope. I didn't even have to read the letter to know what it contained. Mommy's face already said it all.

I stared at the words anyway, trying to absorb what they said. And then, like a straggler catching up in a race, the happiness came. It smacked into me so hard that it almost toppled me over!

I ran to my mother and hugged her as tightly as I could. She hugged me back, saying, "Congratulations, Ora. I hope this school will be just right for you."

I didn't say that I hoped so, too. I already knew that it would be.

✿ ✿ ✿

After that, it was all one big jumble. The final week or two of the school year sped by, bringing with them a few last tests, and then good-bye parties and report cards. I hardly noticed any of it.

On the very last day in my old school, I felt a pang of something like homesickness. Until my friend Gila moved away, I'd been happy here. It wasn't the school's fault that I'd been so *un*happy afterward…

As I walked out of the building for the last time, I sent a silent message: *It's not that I'm choosing to leave you. It's just that I need to be someplace else.*

I hoped it understood.

On my final walk home with Lana and Shoshie, I tried to pay attention to what they were saying. I really did. But how long can you listen to boring talk about clothes and shoes without your eyes glazing over? The answer — for me, at least — was not very long at all.

Soon my mind was wandering far away. I dreamed about next year, and how different everything would be.

I had not told these girls that I was switching schools, partly because I didn't want the bother of explaining why and what and where, and partly because they were too busy talking about their own stuff. On the block before I would wave good-bye for the last time, Lana turned to me and said, "You hardly said a word all the way home, Ora. Are you so sad about school being over?" She laughed heartily at her own joke.

Since it was the last time, I decided to be honest with her for once.

"No," I said. "Just a little bored of the conversation."

I'll never forget the astonishment in her eyes.

Shoshie looked surprised, too. They wouldn't miss me for a minute, those two. I was happy that they had each other... and even happier that those boring walks were finally over with!

As I stepped into my house and closed the door behind me, I had a sense of closing the door on a part of my life, too. Something new was coming up, and I couldn't wait.

But there were two months of summer vacation to get through first. And that meant camp.

Like I'd told Lana, my mother had done most of the shopping for me. The stuff she'd bought was in bags in a corner of my room. The next morning, it was time to get ready in earnest. There was a flurry of packing and last-minute shopping for things like sunscreen and anti-mosquito spray. Then one more Shabbos with my family, followed by hugs and kisses and the drive down to the bus on Sunday morning with my duffels.

I boarded the bus, took a window seat, and lost myself in a daydream all the way up to the mountains.

It was a fine daydream, in which I adored my new school, made a ton of friends, and became a star soloist in the choir, dazzling everyone who heard me sing. Usually, each summer, I strain for my first glimpse of the mountains, with their rich cover of forest green that contrasts so stunningly with the blue sky above.

Not this year. My mind was somewhere else completely. I hardly noticed when we arrived at our destination, and only really woke up when it was time to find my bunkhouse, choose a bed, and get settled in for the season.

The girls in my bunk seemed okay, and I had a feeling that camp would be fine. But this summer would be different from those that came before. I usually enjoy every minute of camp and am sorry when it's over. This year, I was secretly willing the days to move faster.

I couldn't wait to take my place in September as a proud member of JAPA — otherwise known as the Bais Yaakov of Valley Stream!

"*Which* school?" my bunkmates asked in confusion, when we introduced ourselves and shared the names of our schools.

"It's new," I explained patiently. "It's a regular Bais Yaakov, but with something special." And I told them what that something special was.

Some of the girls looked at me with admiration. Others had a look I recognized because I often felt the same way myself: envy.

That made me uncomfortable, so I decided not to talk about school anymore. There was plenty going on in camp to keep me busy without it. Plenty of great activities and good times to be had with my bunkmates.

I settled in to have fun and put September right out of my mind... except after lights-out, when I would pull it out like a favorite treat and munch on it for a few delicious minutes before I fell asleep.

And so, the summer weeks flew by. I'd expected them to drag, but they did just the opposite. I could hardly believe it when it was time to pack up again to go home. I kept taking long, last looks at the trees and the grass and the blue, blue sky, storing them up in my memory until the next time I'd be back in the mountains. I guess you can tell that I'm crazy about nature, but I don't get to see too much of it in the city. That's why I was soaking it up now, while I still could.

Finally, our last breakfast was over, and we were standing by the buses, getting ready to board them for the trip back to the city. There were girls crowded in front of each bus, chattering away while waiting for the driver to open the doors. Suddenly, someone came flying out of a clump of campers, headed in my direction.

When she reached me, she asked breathlessly, "Are you Ora?"

I nodded, curious. Why had she singled me out? I'd seen her around before, in a different bunk of girls my age, but we'd never really talked. She was usually surrounded by her bunkmates and seemed like a cheerful, friendly sort of person. She had curly red hair and sparkling eyes — at least, they were sparkling now.

Her name was Penina, but everyone called her Penny. She said it was because, when she was little, her father said that her hair looked like a bright, new copper penny. And it did!

"Someone just told me that you're going to JAPA!" Penny squealed.

"That's right," I said. "So?"

"So *I'm* going there, too!"

My eyes widened. There were a million things I wanted to say, but I didn't get a chance to say any of them. One of the girls standing in front of the other bus called out, "Penny! The door's opening. Come on — it's time to get our seats!"

"Sorry," Penny told me quickly. "I promised to sit with some girls…" With a quick wave, she started hurrying away. I watched her go, disappointed.

Then she turned her head, so the red curls caught the sun and looked like shiny copper. Over her shoulder she flashed me a big smile and called, "See you in school!"

I felt like pumping my fist. *Yes*!

Chapter 9
New Beginnings

On the night before the first day of school, Abba said, "Get ready, everyone. Mommy and I are taking you all out to dinner!"

"What's the occasion?" Binny asked.

"It's a celebration," my father answered.

"But what are we celebrating?"

"Well, Bassi's about to start high school. Ora's starting a whole new school, too. Huvi's about to start kindergarten. And you're getting ready for a new *year* at school. So we're going out to celebrate… new beginnings!"

"What about Shmulie?"

Abba laughed. "Oops, forgot about him. But don't worry, he won't be left out. Shmulie will be starting a new babysitter next week."

"So *he* can celebrate, too!" Huvi declared.

As the ending days of summer had crept past and the new school year came closer and closer, those pesky butterflies came back for an encore performance, doing their nervous dance in my insides. But they were happy butterflies this time, and it was a happy kind of nervousness. The kind you feel when you're about to embark on an amazing adventure. You don't know exactly what it'll be like, but you can't wait to find out!

"I'll be ready in a sec!" I cried. I dashed up to my room to run a brush through my thick, dark curls. As usual, they didn't look much better when I was finished. But who cared? We were going out for dinner, and school was starting tomorrow!

When we were all assembled at the front door, Abba led the way to the minivan and we climbed inside.

"Where to?" he asked.

Binny shouted out the name of his favorite milchig place. Nobody objected. Soon we were enjoying slices of fresh, hot pizza and fries. Mommy ordered a bowl of ziti for Shmulie, who sat in a highchair picking the pieces of macaroni out of the red sauce one by one and stuffing them into his mouth. My father lifted his cup of soda and said, "To new beginnings!"

We all lifted our cups to touch his. Mommy turned away from the highchair and raised her cup, too. "To new beginnings!"

That was when Shmulie decided that he'd had enough to eat. He crammed one last noodle into his mouth, letting the red sauce drip happily down his chin. Then he picked up his bowl and turned it upside-down on his head. The latest in stylish headwear!

"*Oooh!*" Tomato sauce splattered all over Shmulie, the highchair, and everyone seated anywhere near my baby brother. Including the people at the next table...

I'll pass over the next few minutes. Suffice to say that, with the help of two busboys, a pitcher of water, and about a trillion napkins, Mommy managed to clean up Shmulie, the highchair, and nearly everything else that had been splattered with sauce. The people at the next table were good sports about it all, even though one of the girls there was wearing a white skirt that would never be the same.

I thought about my brand-new uniform on the chair in my room, and fell into a daydream again. I was ready for the waiting to be over. Ready for the new beginning to start. Whatever it might bring...

"By the way," my father said, his voice turning serious in a way that made me come out of my daydream and listen. "I know this is a celebration, but I have something to say to you, Binny."

Binny looked a little worried. "What'd I do now?"

"You went through Mr. Grossbaum's back yard again — when he explicitly asked you not to."

"Oh. That."

"Yes, that. We need to respect our neighbor's wishes, Binny."

"It's not fair! *Everybody* uses the back yards. It's the fastest way to get anywhere!"

"I know that," Abba said patiently. "But you have to take into account what Mr. Grossbaum wants. He says that his flowers keep getting trampled when you boys go through his yard."

"So I'll be careful not to step on them," Binny said eagerly. "Going that way saves so much time! Yitzi, a kid in my class, moved in around the corner from us, and he has the *best* games. And the fastest way to get to his house is by going through the back yards and then through a break in the bushes behind the Feinblums' house. Don't worry," Benny added quickly. "Mrs. Feinblum lets."

"But Mr. Grossbaum *doesn't* let you cross his back lawn," Abba reminded him.

"Please try to be more considerate, Binny," Mommy put in.

Binny shrugged and said that he'd try. I noticed that my brother didn't actually say that he'd *do* it. But Huvi started clamoring for more fries, and Shmulie was about to tip over his tray, which now held a plate of fries and ketchup, and my parents were too busy to notice.

"Anyway," Abba said, when a second disaster had been averted, "I want to wish us all a fantastic year."

"Especially Bassi and Ora," Ma said, smiling at both of us. "It's not easy starting in a whole new school."

"Actually, I'm excited to go," Bassi said.

I was quick to add my voice to hers. "Me, too!"

"Then I guess we have nothing to worry about," my father said. "More pizza, anyone?"

In different homes around the city, other people were looking ahead to a new beginning, too.

Mrs. Mammon was sitting at her dining room table, making a few final changes to the speech she would deliver the next morning, at their very first school assembly. She would greet the girls and explain the school rules and regulations. Most of all, she wanted to share with them her vision of what this unusual new school was all about.

She studied the words she'd written, crossed out a word, and wrote down a better one. It would have been faster to type it on her computer, but for something as important as this speech she wanted to hold a pen in her hand. Her thoughts seemed to be clearer that way.

She changed one more word, and then sat back. There! The speech was ready.

And *she* was ready, too. Ready to lead her beautiful school into what she hoped would be a beautiful future.

Elsewhere in the city, girls like Ora were getting ready for bed, their hearts pattering with excitement and their uniforms folded and ready for the morning.

Some girls were already asleep, dreaming of dancing or singing or playing their favorite instrument. Penny's flute lay on her night table, where she would see it first thing and not forget to put it in her backpack in the morning.

The bus driver had studied his route and was ready to take the girls on the forty-five-minute drive from Brooklyn to Valley Stream.

Miss Reingold, the school secretary, was checking her list of office supplies and wondering if she'd ordered an adequate supply of paper clips and Scotch Tape.

Mr. Katzman, who was in charge of maintenance in the new building, had checked and double-checked to make sure that everything was in the best shape it could be.

And then it was morning. An inviting one, filled with sunshine. They all woke up to greet the new day. An exciting, once-in-a-lifetime kind of day.

The very first day of a brand-new school!

Chapter 10

Starlight

The school building looked even nicer than the first time I'd seen it. The whole outside had been washed clean. Someone had hung up the name of the school on the front brick wall in big, golden letters:

BAIS YAAKOV OF VALLEY STREAM

And, underneath, in slightly smaller letters:

Jewish Academy for the Performing Arts

Fresh flowers had been planted along the front of the building, too: a riot of yellows and purples and pinks, vivid against the smooth green lawn. I was glad that someone had cared about making the school look so inviting. It was a thrill to think that I belonged to this place. I could still hardly believe it!

All around me, girls were standing uncertainly, peeking at each other while pretending not to. Here and there, I saw pairs of girls who knew each other from before, but most of us were strangers to each other.

But there was one girl who was not a total stranger. Off to my right, in the middle of a clump of students in uniform, I spotted a head of red hair. My heart rose — until I saw that the girl's hair was longer than Penny's, and actually closer to auburn than red.

Ever since she ran over to me as we waited to board the bus at camp, I had kept Penny in the back of my mind like a secret treasure. I was so glad to be able to start my first day of school knowing at least one person. And she'd seemed like such a *nice* person, too!

Worried, I checked my watch. It was almost time for school to start. Where was she?

The school bus had turned out not to be a bus at all, but rather a large white van. The ride to Valley Stream had been long, but I didn't really mind. I was feeling a little shy. I guess most of the other girls felt the same way, because we were all quiet, gazing out the windows at the different neighborhoods we passed. I wondered why Penny was not on the van. I wondered where she lived. I wondered if we would become friends this year. The van finally pulled into a smallish parking lot and the driver opened the doors to let us out.

We stood around in front of the school, darting bashful looks at each other and taking it all in. I was swiveling my head from right to left in search of Penny, when I felt a tap on my shoulder.

I spun around — and there she was!

"Hi," Penny said, with the big smile I remembered from camp. "Whew! Glad I made it on time. The traffic was awful!"

"Did your parents drive you?"

She nodded. "They're hoping to find some people to carpool with. I hope that works out."

"Why don't you just take the van, like everyone else?"

The minute the question was out of my mouth, I was sorry I'd asked. Penny's face drooped a little. She said simply, "Too expensive."

I wondered if Penny's family was poor. And, if they were, how her parents could afford to send her here. I knew from listening to my own parents that the tuition was higher than at most other schools, because of the musical training.

But there was no time to wonder about that now. Inside the building, a bell rang. The glass doors opened and there was Mrs. Mammon, smiling at us and looking just the same as I remembered her, only more official.

"Come in, girls." Somehow, she managed to make herself heard without raising her voice. There was a stampede toward the door, but with the principal standing there we managed to get inside more or less decorously.

"Go straight to the auditorium, please," she announced. "We'll be davening together, followed by an assembly."

My pulse pounded madly. This was it! My first morning, my first davening, my first assembly.

Best of all, Penny was right beside me as I slipped into the rows indicated for the seventh graders. She stayed with me so naturally, as if we were old friends instead of a couple of girls who'd hardly said two words to each other before in our lives.

Sitting in that auditorium on the first day of school, with Penny next to me... well, there's just no other way to say it. I was on top of the world!

When davening ended, Mrs. Mammon climbed the stairs to the stage and took her place in front of the podium. The room quieted as we all stopped talking and started listening.

"Welcome, girls," she said, her eyes sweeping along the rows of seats so that she seemed to be talking to each one of us personally. "Welcome to the Bais Yaakov of Valley Stream. Otherwise known as... JAPA. Jewish Academy for the Performing Arts!" She paused as we broke into a spontaneous cheer. It took quite a while for us to settle down. I guess everyone was feeling as excited as I was. And I was so excited that I could hardly sit still!

When the auditorium was finally silent again, Mrs. Mammon continued. "As you know, we are a special kind of school. Something different."

We were about to erupt in cheers again, but the principal held up a hand for quiet.

Mrs. Mammon went on to explain the kind of schedule we would have. Apart from the usual *limudei kodesh* and secular subjects, there would be either voice training, musical training, or dancing classes for every girl in the school.

"We are not simply going to be a school that *happens* to have a dance group, or a choir, or a band. We are going to be professionals! When an organization approaches us and asks us to perform, they will know that they're getting the highest caliber talent available among *frum* junior and high-school girls today."

Another cheer, and some loud applause. We were glowing with anticipation, and with pride, too. We wanted exactly what Mrs. Mammon wanted — to be the best of the best!

"But being a fine performer is not enough," she warned. "You will be expected to keep up with your schoolwork, just like students in any other school. Musical training and rehearsals notwithstanding, there will be no slouching off."

There was a stir at this. Then we settled down and paid attention again.

"In the outside world," Mrs. Mammon said, looking suddenly very solemn, "many people dream of being a 'star.' They want to be famous, to attract attention, to be praised and admired." Even from my seat in the middle of the room, I could see the intensity in the principal's eyes.

"You girls will be praised and admired, too. In a way, you're going to be stars. But it's very important that you understand the difference between a Jewish 'star' and the kind that the world talks about."

We were listening very closely now. You could have heard a pin drop in that auditorium. When someone on the other side of the room coughed, I nearly jumped.

"What do real stars do up in the sky? They shed light on the world. And that," she told us, "is the kind of stars that we are hoping to produce here. We want girls who will perform so that people can receive the help they need. We want girls who are not interested in getting attention for themselves, but rather in spreading light and joy to others.

"Girls," she ended forcefully, "who take the special 'starlight' that Hashem has given them — and shower it onto the world around them!"

This time, there was no cheering. Instead, a respectful hush fell over the big room… as if our thoughts were too deep to be expressed in words or applause. Mrs. Mammon seemed pleased by our reaction. It meant we were taking what she'd said seriously.

Suddenly, she clapped her hands together and cried, "*Hatzlachah*, girls! And now, it's time to go to your classrooms. Classes begin in exactly five minutes!"

With a roar of voices all talking at once, we rose and headed for the auditorium doors. My head was still whirling with the impact of Mrs. Mammon's speech, but I would think about that later. Right now, I hurried as quickly as the crowd would allow. I had five minutes to find the seventh-grade classroom, and I had no idea which one it was.

"Wait up, Ora," Penny gasped behind me. "Let's not get separated in the crowd. I don't want to lose you."

I felt the exact same way. Losing Penny was the last thing I wanted. I stopped and let the others swarm past me as I waited for her to catch up.

Two minutes later, we were walking together into the seventh-grade classroom.

Chapter 11

First Impressions

Penny-Chaya-Gali-Devori-Layala-Esti-Fraidy-Ruthie-Nomi-Aviva-Ricki.

The names of my new classmates ran together in my mind like one long name. How would I ever manage to sort them out?

In my old school, I'd known most of the girls in my class since kindergarten. Here, they were all new faces. Totally new people who would soon become the center of my world.

But right now — except for Penny — they were still just faces. And names. *Devori-Layala-Gali-Fraidy-Chaya-Esti-Ruthie-Aviva-Ricki-Nomi.*

One or two girls did stand out. Aviva — or was it Esti? — had a long, thick braid down her back. Devori (at least, I *think* it was Devori) had eyes that were as green as a cat's. Chaya had a heart-shaped face, huge blue eyes, and shiny brown hair to frame it all. There was a kind of gentleness about her that was different from the other girls. Catching my eye, she gave me a shy smile. I smiled back and quickly looked away.

Since we were such a small class — only twelve of us altogether — Morah Gunner had decided not to seat us in the usual rows. Instead, our desks were arranged in a semi-circle facing the teacher's desk. That way, each of us could see the others, and Morah could see everyone.

I was a little scared of Morah Gunner at first. She didn't smile as she introduced herself. My sister once told me that some teachers are extra-strict at the start of a new school year but ease up as the year goes on. I hoped that would happen here. I sat with my spine extra straight, trying to pay attention. Hoping to make a good first impression.

That first class seemed to move very slowly. Maybe that was because it was all so new. Still unsmiling, Morah Gunner outlined her rules and discussed the kind of tests we would have. She told us about the homework we could expect and what would happen if we didn't complete our assignments.

Then she told us to take out our Chumashim — and something surprising happened. The minute she started teaching, the sternness dropped away. She looked and sounded happy and enthusiastic as she went through the *pesukim*. As if she loved this so much that she just couldn't help it.

Maybe having Morah Gunner as my main teacher would be okay, after all...

After that, everything started speeding up. We had two more classes, and then a short break for recess. Penny stuck close to me at first, but she was such a friendly person that we weren't alone in the school yard for long. With her big smile, she made everyone feel comfortable right away and was soon laughing and talking with our classmates.

I joined in the conversations, too, even though the person I really wanted to talk to was Penny. I wanted to get to know her better.

But so, it seemed, did everybody else.

It's hard to explain what Penny had. It was something that drew people to her like a magnet. A kind of *sparkle* is the best way I can put it. Not the kind of sparkle that you put on to make people notice you. Penny's sparkle was part of her. It was who she was. She was simply — sparkly!

We sat together at lunch, and a few other girls joined us at our table. Then came the afternoon, when we were divided into different tracks for subjects like math and English. Penny and I were not in all the same classes, so I didn't get to see her much. We spent afternoon recess in our own classrooms because it started drizzling, but by the time the last bell rang the sky was clear again.

"Girls! Go down to the lobby to check the bulletin board outside the office door," the school secretary's voice boomed over the intercom. "Find your name and see where you need to go for music prep." That's what they called the performing-arts part of our school: "music prep." Later, as we got nearer to a performance, it would change to "rehearsals."

I felt that shiver down my back again. I almost tripped over my own feet as I hurried down the stairs with the others to find my name on the bulletin board. I was to go to Room 8.

"I'm so excited!" squealed a voice in my ear. It was Penny. I was glad to see her again.

"Where do *you* go?" I asked.

"The band meets in Room 6," she said. "And I think the dancers use the auditorium."

The voice over the intercom announced, "There will be a short break before music prep. Please be in your assigned rooms in ten minutes."

There were a lot of girls in the lobby, their voices loud and excited. How different from that morning, when we were still complete strangers to each other! Penny and I considered going outside on the lawn but weren't sure if we were allowed to. Finally, we decided to go down one flight of stairs to the basement level, where it was much quieter than the lobby. I wanted to hear all about her afternoon classes, and she wanted to hear about mine.

We settled on the floor, with our backs to the wall near what I assumed was a janitor's closet, both of us talking a mile a minute.

"So how do you like this place so far?" Penny asked.

"I love it! You?"

"Everything except the homework. We got *tons* of it — especially in math. On the first day of school!" Penny pulled a woebegone face that made me laugh.

"If you need help with the math," I said, "you can ask me." I was in the high track in math and Penny wasn't.

Her eyes grew round. "What, you actually *like* math?"

I shrugged. "I happen to be pretty good with numbers."

We fell silent for a few seconds. That's when we heard

a strange thumping. It was coming from somewhere nearby. Had it been going on all along, only we'd been talking too much to hear?

We stared at each other. If Penny's eyes were round before, they were like saucers now.

"What's that?" she whispered.

"I don't know. Could it be… mice?"

"Mice don't make so much noise. Don't you know the expression, 'Quiet as a mouse'?"

"Well, what is it, then?"

"I don't know. But I think it's coming from in there." She pointed at the janitor's closet.

We struggled to our feet and tiptoed closer to the closet door. She was right. The thumping was definitely coming from in there.

I glanced at Penny. She looked scared.

I was scared, too — but I was even more curious. Also, I was a little mad at whatever was in there, scaring us. Without letting myself stop to think, I put my hand on the doorknob and yanked with all my might.

The door swung open…

…and somebody fell out!

She came out backward, arms wheeling frantically as she tried to keep her balance. No use. She crashed into me and both of us toppled right over.

I managed to prop myself up on one elbow and stare at the girl's face, or as much of it as I could see from the tangled heap we were in. She looked vaguely familiar. The girl stared back at me, eyes wide with surprise at our unexpected encounter.

Penny gaped at the girl, too. Then she started laughing. "*Gali*? Is that you?"

As we both hauled ourselves into a sitting position, I finally got to see the girl right-side-up. I recognized her, too. I'd seen her in Mrs. Gunner's class that morning, and she'd been in my math class in the afternoon. Gali was on the tall side, with long, thin arms and legs, a long blond ponytail, and big, brown eyes. She rubbed her elbow, looking abashed.

"What," I asked crossly, "were you doing in that closet?" I rubbed my shoulder, which had bumped hard on the basement floor when I fell.

Gingerly, she shook her arms and legs as if making sure they still worked. "I needed someplace quiet where I could stretch."

"Stretch? In that tiny closet?"

"It's actually much bigger than it looks on the outside," Gali explained. "It's kind of narrow, but goes back a pretty long way."

"Isn't it full of buckets and mops and things?" Penny asked.

Gali shook her head. "Nope. Right now, it's empty."

"So you decided to go inside and stretch," I prompted. I wanted to hear the rest of the story.

"That's right. Did you know that stretching is the most important part of exercising?"

"I guess so. But why now?"

"Because I have dance practice in a few minutes, and I wanted to warm up first."

Understanding dawned. Gali was one of the students whose special talent was dancing. I nodded my head. Beside me, Penny murmured, "Got it."

"Well," Gali said, standing up and brushing herself off. When she moved, she was like a rubber band, bending easily any which way. Graceful, too. "Nice to bump into you, I guess."

At the exact same second, Penny and I both remembered how she'd looked when she came flying backward out of the closet. We burst into peals of laughter. After a surprised second, Gali laughed, too.

A new voice came from the stairs, slicing into our laughter and cutting it off.

"Oh, forget it," the voice drawled. "We'd better look for someplace else. This place is occupied by *babies*."

I looked up. Two girls stood halfway down the flight of stairs from the lobby. Ninth graders, by the look of them.

"Who's a baby?" I demanded. "We're in seventh grade!"

The girl snorted. A second later, so did her friend. But before either of them could say another word, the secretary was back on the intercom. "Two minutes to music prep, girls."

The two ninth graders turned and disappeared the way they'd come.

"Help! We'll be late!" With a terrified look, Gali scrambled to her feet. She was halfway up the stairs before Penny and I had even started moving.

Chapter 12

One Tiny Mosquito

I couldn't have been happier as I burst through the door of Room 8 for my very first voice training session. Or was it choir practice? Whichever it was, I was ready to love it.

I felt like a fish that had been gasping for breath in the open air and finally, finally, gets to slide back into a pond of cool, refreshing water — her real world.

As I sat at a desk waiting for the choir director to come in, I had flashes of memory from last year in my old school. I remembered how lonely I'd felt, even when I was with Lana and Shoshie. Like a fish out of water!

Here, I felt comfortable.

Here, I could sing.

Here, I could shine!

I looked around at my fellow singers. There were three girls from my own class — Chaya, who in my opinion was definitely the prettiest girl in our class, Ruthie, who had braces, and Devori with the long braid — plus others from the eighth and ninth grades whose names I didn't know yet. Everyone around me was a stranger, but hopefully that wouldn't last long. Soon I would know them all. I would know their names, and their voices, and the way they sang. And they would know the same things about me...

Right now, we were all sitting near the girls we knew best — our own classmates. I sat between Ruthie and Devori, with Chaya on Ruthie's other side.

When we were all assembled in the room, the door opened one last time, and in walked the young woman with the big glasses who'd auditioned me. She walked energetically, as if she couldn't wait to get started.

"Hi, all!" she greeted us cheerfully. "Welcome to our choir! I am Miss Sperling, and I'll be teaching you songs for our very first performance!"

She seemed to speak with a lot of exclamation points. I decided that I liked her.

An eighth or ninth grader — I think her name was Dina — asked eagerly, "When's the first performance?"

Miss Sperling smiled mysteriously. "That's for me to know and you to find out..."

But there was something in the way she said it that told us she was joking. We all began clamoring for her to tell us, and pretty soon, she did.

"This Chanukah," she said in a thrilling voice, "we hope to put on a small performance just for your mothers, grandmothers, and sisters. A few other special guests will be invited, too. That way, your families can get a sense of what we're trying to do here. And it'll also give others in the community — and beyond — a chance to hear about us and to watch us in action."

There was a buzz of excitement. Miss Sperling held up a hand.

"The first thing we're going to do today," she said, "is check out your voices. I need to know which group to put each of you in — alto, soprano, and so forth."

And so forth? I raised my hand. "I thought there's just two groups, soprano and alto."

"No way." Miss Sperling laughed. "Officially, there is a range of six or seven voices that girls can have — starting from soprano, the highest, down to contralto, the deepest. In between are things like alto and mezzo-soprano, to name two." She turned to the girl closest to the door and said, "Let's start with you and go around the room."

The girl asked nervously, "What do I do?"

"First tell us who you are and what grade you're in. And then — sing." Miss Sperling named a popular Jewish song. "I want to hear your range."

The girl introduced herself as Chava Sara, in the eighth grade. As soon as she started singing, I was sure Miss Sperling would put her in the soprano group. Her voice was high and clear.

But Miss Sperling said, "Mezzo-soprano." She made a notation in her notebook and then motioned for the next girl to take her turn.

As we went around the room, I tried to guess which group each girl belonged in. After a while, I got pretty good at it. When it was my turn, I belted out the song just the way I'd done at my audition. My voice filled the room, and then some. Miss Sperling nodded happily. "A powerful alto," she murmured, and wrote it down in her notebook.

I beamed. Out of the whole group, it was possible that I had the best voice. It was true, and it was strong. Powerful, Miss Sperling had called it.

The last girl to sing was Chaya, my classmate. She looked a little bashful as she stood up, took a breath and started to sing. When I heard her voice, it was hard not to stare.

Her voice climbed into the air like a — what's the name of that bird that sings at dusk? — a nightingale. Every note was clear and liquid and perfect. We listened, spellbound, until the last note died away. And then, spontaneously, we broke into applause.

I clapped along with the others, even though my heart was sinking so fast that it made me dizzy.

"Wonderful," Miss Sperling said, beaming. "You're a soprano for sure."

Chaya was not only a soprano — she was the best soprano I'd ever heard! Suddenly my own voice, which I'd been so proud of just moments before, seemed paltry compared to hers. Second-best.

Was it always going to be my fate to play second fiddle?

The thought flew around me like an annoying mosquito at a picnic. One tiny mosquito, to ruin all the fun.

A minute ago, I'd been on top of the world. But now… Well, remember how I told you about my moods?

Hearing Chaya sing, I went from high-C down to D-flat in no time at all.

We spent the rest of the session learning the first part

of a song that we would be performing on Chanukah. Next time, Miss Sperling said, we would be introduced to the harmony. I liked the song, and I liked the way Miss Sperling seemed to enjoy my voice.

The problem was, she obviously enjoyed Chaya's even more.

One tiny mosquito, whining and whining around my head to destroy my happiness.

Chapter 13

Sooo Special

By the time choir practice was over, the mosquito had quieted down some. It was still buzzing around at the back of my head, but I could ignore it. I was tired and hungry and more than ready to go home.

We took our backpacks out to the parking lot. Mrs. Mammon was there to see us off. Had it only been that morning when I'd stood in this very spot with a bunch of strangers, wondering what the day would bring? It felt like something that had happened a long, long time ago. Yawning, I looked around for Penny.

She was standing at the other end of the lot, waiting for her parents to come get her. About six other girls were standing there, too. Seeing me, she broke into a smile and waved. I waved back, glad that she was happy to see me but sorry that we weren't going home together. The long drive would have been a perfect time to get better acquainted.

Lots of people were talking, but one voice stood out above the rest. Turning, I saw one of the girls who had stood at the top of the basement steps before music prep. The ninth grader who had taken one look at us and called us "babies."

She stood with her friend and a few other girls, not far away from where I was waiting to board the van. I don't know what they were talking about, but she suddenly flung out her arms and spun around, graceful as a ballerina.

"We," she sang out in a ringing voice, "are *sooo* special…"

Her friends laughed. One of them called out, "And *you're* more special than most. Right, Shayna?"

"But of course." She gave a low bow, and they laughed again.

On the other side of the lot was another familiar figure. It was Gali. She was bending and stretching as if she were alone in her room at home. Or in the janitor's closet in the basement. I guess she took her post-dance stretches just as seriously as she took her pre-dance ones.

Some of the other girls gave her a funny look, but she just ignored them and kept on doing what she was doing. I wanted to wave, but she was too busy stretching to see me.

It turned out that there was more than just one van taking us to and from school. There were three of them, to cover different neighborhoods. They were lined up in a row now, waiting for us to get on board. I found the one that said "Flatbush" and climbed on along with the girls I'd ridden in with that morning.

This time, I recognized some of the faces. Esti, Fraidy, and Layala were in my class. We took seats together somewhere near the middle of the van.

Then I saw another face I recognized. My heart sank. Shayna.

I prayed that she wouldn't recognize me the way I'd recognized her. But I guess she hadn't taken a very good look at the seventh-grade "babies" down in the basement earlier, because she sailed past me without a second glance.

The van rumbled out of the parking lot. My classmates and I compared notes about school for a while. Then our words gradually petered out until they stopped altogether. I guess we were all tired.

The motion of the wheels was soothing, and the sound of the cars moving past on the highway was like a lullaby. I'm pretty sure I dozed off for a while. Maybe some of the other girls did, too.

When I opened my eyes again and looked out the window, the streets were familiar. The stores were familiar, too.

In no time at all, we were turning down a block that looked *very* familiar.

Home.

My short nap had left me fizzing with energy again. I couldn't wait to tell my mother all about my day. I wanted to tell her every single thing, starting with the principal's speech at our assembly and all the way through my very first choir practice.

I burst through the front door, dumped my backpack, and ran straight to the kitchen, where I thought I heard her voice. "Mommy!"

Sure enough, my mother was there. So was Bassi. They were sitting at the table and laughing their heads off about something.

I waited until they could hear me, and then asked, "What's the joke?"

Mommy looked at me, but she didn't seem to *see* me. She was still smiling broadly at whatever she'd been laughing about with my sister. "You won't believe it! Bassi's Navi teacher turns out to be an old school friend of mine!"

"Really? How exciting." *Not.*

"Mommy's old friend still has the same sense of humor that she had when she and Mommy were girls," Bassi said, eager to fill me in. "When I described some of the funny things she said, Mommy said that she hadn't changed a bit!"

This was all very fascinating, but not exactly what I wanted to be talking about just then. I waited for someone to ask me how *my* day had been, but my mother had started laughing again. "I *must* give her a call and tell her how happy I am that she'll be teaching you this year..."

"I'm sure she'll be thrilled to hear from you," Bassi agreed. Then she said something I didn't get, but which Mommy thought was hysterical. Probably another one of her old friend's jokes. They were both rolling again.

I looked from Mommy to Bassi, wondering when anyone would remember that I existed. I, who had just spent my very first day in a brand-new and one-of-a-kind school.

I pictured Shayna, twirling around in the parking lot and saying, "We are soooo special!" Everyone had laughed, but it was true. We *were* special!

I was special!

Why couldn't anyone around here seem to remember that?

Mommy wiped the corners of her eyes with the tip of her apron. "Oh, my! I haven't had such a good laugh in ages." She stood up, went to the oven, and pulled open the door to check on whatever was cooking there. Then she straightened up and turned back around.

"Hi, Ora!" she said, smiling at me as if she'd just noticed me for the first time. "How was *your* first day of school?"

Suddenly, I did not feel like talking about it anymore. Not while Mommy still had her old friend — Bassi's Navi teacher — on her mind. Not with the echo of their laughter still hanging in the room.

You'd think that my own mother would be eager to hear every last detail of my first day at JAPA. But no. She was more interested in Bassi. As usual.

I gritted my teeth. I wanted my days of being second fiddle to be over. *Gone.*

"It was fine," I muttered.

And I clumped out of the kitchen and up to my room.

It wasn't until supper that I finally filled in the family about my day at school.

Mommy asked me questions, and so did Abba. Bassi seemed fascinated by everything I had to say. Even Binny paid attention for a few minutes, which was quite flattering considering his usual attention span, which is down near zero.

When I paused for breath, Abba turned to my brother. "How about you, Binny? How's the new year going so far?"

Before Binny could answer, I'd filled my lungs with air and was ready for more. "We started learning our first song today — for a performance on Chanukah!" I announced importantly. I'd already described my teachers, my classes, my classmates, and my choir. "The melody is gorgeous, but the harmony is going to be really hard. Miss Sperling says that I'm a 'powerful alto.' I think she likes my voice."

"That's wonderful, dear," Mommy said.

"Yes!" Bassi agreed enthusiastically.

"Good to hear," Abba said.

Huvi asked, "Are you going to be famous?"

I smiled graciously at her and said, "Who knows? Maybe."

"Okay, let's not get any swelled heads around here." My father grinned.

I heard him, but I didn't really listen to what he was saying. It felt too good to be the center of attention. To have my parents and my perfect big sister hanging on my every word.

(*We are soooo special…*)

I was flying. On top of the world. This was what I'd been waiting for all my life! To feel exactly the way I did right now.

Of course, it didn't last.

An hour later, as I was sitting at my desk doing some math problems, I got a call from Penny.

A call that brought that miserable mosquito whining around me again — full force.

Chapter 14

Out in the Cold

Mommy called up the stairs, "Ora! Call for you!" I ran for the phone, hoping against hope that it would be Penny. And it was!

I was overjoyed. "Hi!" I said into the phone.

"Hi!" The sound of Penny's sunny voice instantly filled me with — well, with sunshine. We talked fast, tumbling over our words, trying to catch up on the news since we'd last seen each other.

"How was band practice?" I asked, after telling her all about my choir.

"It was amazing! Though Mrs. Judowitz — she's our music teacher — prefers to call it the *orchestra*. She thinks it's classier."

"How can an eight-piece band be an orchestra?"

"Mrs. Judowitz is hoping that we'll have more instruments eventually. She's got all sorts of plans!"

"Okay... So how was *orchestra* practice?"

"Amazing! We have someone on the electronic keyboard, two electric guitars, a clarinet, a saxophone, a cello, and two flutes — including me. We're still getting used to each other, but I can tell that we're going to sound awesome!"

"Did Mrs. Judowitz tell you about the performance on Chanukah?"

"She sure did. I can't wait!"

"Me, neither…"

We were talking about the performance when there was a sudden commotion at Penny's end. "Whoa! Just a second…" she said. I heard voices talking, screeching, and laughing. It sounded like a circus over there!

Finally, Penny got back on the phone. Laughing, she said, "You will not *believe* what my brother just did!"

She was talking about her brother Zevi, who was apparently five years old.

"He decided that he wanted to make brownies, but he didn't have a clue how! He figured it was mostly chocolate, so he poured *five bags* of chocolate chips into the blender, along with some water… and he forgot to cover the blender. Now our nice, clean kitchen has chocolate-covered walls!" Penny giggled. "I should send a picture to one of those interior-design magazines. We'll win first prize for sure!"

"Poor you," I said, laughing along with her.

"Poor Zevi. He never got to have his brownies!"

"Do you have to help clean it up?" I asked.

"Nah. I have three older sisters who usually end up doing stuff like that."

"Three older sisters? Any brothers?"

"Yup. Three of them. And," Penny added, "three *younger* sisters."

I quickly added up in my head. "That makes... ten in all?"

"Yup."

"Wow!"

"Double wow," Penny said placidly. "Our house is bursting at the seams, my mother says. She and my father are always talking about how we need a bigger house, but everyone's too busy to go look for one."

I pictured a house made of cloth, with beds and tables and chairs oozing out of the seams like stuffing. That made me giggle again. But the giggles dried up fast when Penny dropped her bombshell.

"Oh, I forgot to tell you. Great news!"

"What?"

"Remember how I said that my parents wished they could find someone nearby who'd be interested in carpooling with us? Well, they did! Now they'll only have to drive me to and from school *half* the time."

"That's great!" I said. "So who'll you be carpooling with?"

"That's the best part," Penny said happily. "It's a girl from our own class."

Somehow, I knew. Even before she said the name, I could have said it for her.

"It's Chaya!" Penny squealed. "Turns out she lives just a few blocks away. Isn't that amazing?"

"A...mazing," I agreed weakly.

Stunning Chaya, with her out-of-this-world voice, would now be traveling to and from school with Penny every single school day of the year. Getting to know her better. Getting closer to her every day.

While I would be — where?

Exactly nowhere.

Out in the cold.

Why couldn't anything ever go right for me? It just wasn't fair! I fumed in my room until Bassi came up to do her homework, and then I went downstairs to fume some more.

Penny was the kind of girl who liked pretty much everyone. That was part of what I liked about *her*. I didn't blame her for wanting to be friends with Chaya — or Chaya for wanting to be friends with her.

It was just that I'd waited so long to have a best friend that I'd almost forgotten how nice it was. And I'd been hoping that Penny would be it.

I wouldn't have minded if someone else had been Penny's carpool partner. But why did it have to be *Chaya*?

Why did it have to be another one of those "perfect people," like my sister? Someone with a voice I could never compete with. Someone who made me feel like I'd never be more than a runner-up. A second fiddle.

A tiny voice kept trying to remind me that Chaya was a nice girl — someone that *I* might like to be friends with, too. But my jealousy did a great job of drowning out that voice. Just the way it always did…

I was slamming around the living room, feeling very sorry for myself, when I suddenly had an idea. A brilliant one!

I ran to the kitchen, but Mommy wasn't there. I finally tracked her down in the basement.

The basement was cooler than the rest of the house, and quieter. Almost like a world all its own. I went through the main room, with the big freezer, the shelves of games and toys, the pull-out couch, and the table hockey that Binny likes to play with his friends, until I reached the laundry room at the rear. Mommy was standing at a big folding table, sorting laundry.

"Ma! I just had a fantastic idea!"

My mother held up one of Binny's shirts and frowned. "Hm?"

"You know that van you have to pay for? The one that takes me to and from school?"

"Yes. What about it?"

"How about saving all that money and doing a carpool instead?"

My mother put down the shirt and stared at me. "Carpool?"

"Sure! I have a friend — Penny from camp, remember? — whose parents drive her to school instead of taking the van. And now another classmate is joining in so they can carpool together. Why not make it a *three*-way carpool? Then you'd only have to drive a few times a week!"

"That," Mommy said firmly, "would be a few times too many."

I blinked. "What?"

"Both your father and I have jobs that would make it very difficult for us to make the long drive out to Valley Stream. That's why we decided to send you on the van in the first place."

"But the van is expensive! Carpooling would cost much less, wouldn't it?"

"I appreciate your concern," my mother said, picking up the shirt again and spraying something on the collar. "But don't worry about it, Ora. *Baruch Hashem*, we can afford to send you by van. There's no need to carpool."

I turned away, dejected. Maybe my parents didn't need a carpool, but *I* sure did.

It was no use. I was going to have to keep on taking the van, while Penny and Chaya traveled to and from school together every single weekday. Pretty soon, Penny would probably forget all about me.

It was almost enough to make me wish I'd never switched schools in the first place.

Almost — but not quite. Penny or no Penny, I still had my beloved choir...

Until I almost didn't.

But that part comes later.

Chapter 15
Problems

I was still in a bad mood when Bassi came up to get ready for bed. All I wanted was to be left alone. I *needed* to be left alone. I knew myself well enough to know that a good night's sleep would smooth out the edges of my mood, leaving me feeling much calmer by morning.

But I knew that my sister was not going to leave me alone. Even before she said a word, I could tell that she was planning to talk. I could almost *hear* her thinking about what to say to me.

For some reason, Bassi always thinks it's her responsibility to cheer me up. She must have seen something of my mood on my face, because she was at her nicest tonight.

"So, tell me more about your amazing choir," she invited, picking up her brush. Bassi brushes her hair every night until it shines… unlike yours truly, who doesn't bother. I tidy my hair in the morning but don't care if it looks like a curly crow's nest by the time I go to bed.

But even a chance to talk about the choir didn't cheer me up. In fact, it made me even grumpier. I remembered how much I'd wanted to tell Mommy about the choir when I came home from school, and how she'd only wanted to hear the things that *Bassi* was telling her. As usual, I'd stood there feeling like I was the less important one. The second fiddle.

"As if you're even interested," I glowered.

"Of course I am!" My sister stared at me in astonishment. "Why would you think I'm not?"

I *knew* I shouldn't say it. I knew I should stop right there and keep the ugly words inside.

But something was pushing me to speak. To give her an inkling of what it felt like to be me: the girl with the perfect big sister. The girl who always came second. The girl who was about to lose her only friend in school.

"Maybe," I said meanly, "you don't want to hear because…"

"Because what?"

"Because you're jealous."

"Jealous?" Bassi's face went blank with surprise. "Me?"

"Yeah. Jealous that *you're* in an ordinary school, while I go to JAPA. I'll get to train my voice, and have choir practice every day, and perform in front of thousands of people…"

"But I'm *not* jealous," she protested. "I'm happy for you, Ora. Really."

I found that hard to believe. I said so out loud. "I find that hard to believe."

For the first time, Bassi looked insulted. "I'm sorry it's so hard for you to believe," she said stiffly. "Why in the world should I wish I were you? I'm happy with my own life, thank you very much."

I crossed my arms skeptically across my chest and huffed, "Hah!"

It takes a lot to make my sister angry, but she was starting to get that way now. There were bright pink splotches of color on both of her cheeks. Her eyebrows came together with a snap. "You think I'm lying? That I really wish I could go to your school?"

I gave a condescending shrug. "Wouldn't anyone?"

At that point, my sister was so furious that she stopped talking. That is unusual for Bassi — being furious, I mean, and not talking to me. Usually, whenever we have a tiff, it's like a storm that blows up and blows over before you know it.

Not this time.

Tonight, Bassi kept wearing a scowl for a long time after she stopped talking. I pretended to fall asleep but kept my eyes slitted, half-open, watching her. Wondering if she was still mad, or if she would say anything else.

I was nearly asleep for real when I heard my sister get up and start moving around the room. Without saying a word, I could tell that she was still mad. She stood in front of the mirror for a few seconds, glaring at my reflection.

Then my sister turned around and walked out the door.

Chapter 16

More Problems

Bassi went into the living room, where she could be alone. Or so she thought.

"Hey!" she said, startled. "What are you doing here?"

The room had looked empty at first. And it *was* empty —except for Binny, slouched in a corner of the couch with both arms wrapped around a cushion crushed against his middle. His answer to her question was a shrug.

Bassi sat down next to him. "Aren't you supposed to be in bed?"

Another shrug.

She studied her brother's face. It did not look happy. She had come down here to brood about her own problems — or rather, her one big problem. A problem named Ora...

But she couldn't ignore the gloom on Binny's face. "Is something wrong?" she asked.

"Wrong?" Binny exploded. "You can say that again!" He hunched even more deeply into his cushion, as if he wished he could disappear into it.

"If you tell me about it, maybe I can help."

He shook his head. "Nobody can help. Except maybe Abba. But he won't."

"Okay." Bassi was getting curiouser by the minute. "Please tell me anyway, Binny. You'll feel better if you get it off your chest."

After another brief hesitation, Binny decided that she was probably right. It sure didn't feel very good keeping his feelings all bottled up inside. Might as well talk and see if it helped any.

So he said, "Remember Mr. Grossbaum?"

"Our neighbor?"

"Yeah."

"Sure, I remember. Abba spoke to you about him when we went out for pizza that night. What about him?"

"You know how all the kids like to cross his back yard to get places, cuz it's quicker?"

Bassi nodded.

"And remember how Abba said that Mr. Grossbaum doesn't want us doing that, cuz it ruins his flowers?"

She nodded again. "So?"

"So I missed out on playing at Yitzi's house today. All because of him!"

Slowly, in fits and starts, the story came out. Yitzi was a cool boy in Binny's class whose family had recently moved in around the corner from the Weisses. Yitzi had all the best games — and, just this week, his father had installed a basketball hoop.

"Yitzi said that I could come over after school with some other kids, to shoot hoops." At nine and a half, Binny was just learning how to throw a basketball and he relished any chance to practice.

"So?" Bassi asked again.

"So I didn't want to go through Mr. Grossbaum's yard and get yelled at again. Instead, I went *aaall* the way around the block." Binny made it sound as if he'd made a journey of a thousand miles instead of just around the corner. "And when I *finally* got to Yitzi's house, the other kids were already in the middle of a game, and Yitzi said I had to wait. And by the time I *finished* waiting, it was suppertime and I had to go home." He scowled. "It's not fair!"

Bassi's heart went out to her brother. "That's tough."

He nodded, his face a grim mask.

"Maybe Abba could ask Mr. Grossbaum if you have permission to walk very carefully around his flower beds?"

Binny shook his head. "Mr. Grossbaum will *never* let."

He sat back, clutching his cushion and picturing endless days of missing games with his friends because he had to take the long way around.

"That's tough," Bassi said again, sympathetically. "I wish I could help."

"No one can help," Binny said again.

"Well, it might help to get a good night's sleep."

She expected him to lash out at her suggestion, and tell her to leave him alone. Instead, to her surprise, he actually got off the couch and said in a forlorn voice, "Guess so." He suddenly sounded younger than his age.

He sounded like a kid whose life was hard and who didn't have much hope that it would be getting easier any time soon.

"Good night, Binny. Sleep tight."

"Yeah. Whatever."

Bassi watched her younger brother start up the stairs until he was out of sight.

And then it was her turn to sit on the couch and brood about *her* problems.

Or rather, her one big problem.

Ora.

Chapter 17

A Cut Above

After Bassi left the room, I realized that I wasn't going to be falling asleep anytime soon. I sat up, turned on the light, and started reading. By the time she came back I was getting drowsy, but the opening door made me feel wide awake again. Was my sister still mad?

Bassi spent the next few minutes getting ready for bed while I read my book, both of us carefully not talking to each other.

We spent the next fifteen minutes reading in bed and *still* not talking to each other.

Finally, Bassi turned off her light.

I turned mine off, too.

Considering what a long and exhausting day I'd had, I expected to drop off right away this time. Instead, I lay wide awake but pretending to sleep. I didn't want my sister to know how rattled I was by our fight. I couldn't believe how calmly *she* was sleeping after the scene we'd just had.

It wasn't until the next day that I began to wonder if Bassi hadn't been pretending, too.

When I saw her drooping over her bowl of cereal in the morning, she sure didn't look like she'd had much sleep the night before. There were bags under her eyes, and her usual zip was definitely missing.

Mommy said good morning to both of us, but we didn't say a word to each other. It felt weird not to be on speaking terms with my own sister. I also felt a little guilty, since *I* was the reason Bassi hadn't slept well. Because of me, Bassi would have to drag herself through her second day of high school only half-awake.

I was tired, too. I knew it wasn't a good idea to go to school without breakfast, so I forced myself to eat something. I was spooning up some instant oatmeal and considering whether or not to say something to Bassi to clear the air, when Binny called from the living room, "I see a van coming up the street, Ora. I think it's yours!"

The van was early! Galvanized, I rushed to get my stuff together and then ran out of the house with a hasty "Bye!" tossed over my shoulder.

In an instant, Bassi was forgotten.

And so was everything else, except for JAPA.

It's amazing how quickly you can get used to things.

As the rest of that first week went by, the sight of Penny and Chaya getting out of a car together in the mornings, and then waiting together again for a car to pick them up at the end of the day, became almost commonplace. I didn't *like* it, but it didn't make me grind my teeth as much, either.

The reason it was easier than I'd expected was because Penny continued to act just the same toward me: nice and friendly. We spent most of the day together, except for math, and we never seemed to run out of things to talk about. After a while, I began to forget that there had ever been a time when she was not a part of my life. I could hardly even remember the time before she ran up to me on the last day of camp to say hi.

From that first minute, I'd liked the way Penny brightened up my day and made me laugh. I liked her big smile and her friendly ways. Chaya was a quieter girl, but I could see how, little by little, Penny was getting her to open up. At first, whenever I saw them together waiting for their ride, it would be Penny who was doing most of the talking. After a while, though, Chaya was doing plenty of it, too. I couldn't help wishing that I knew what they were talking about...

Meanwhile, my classes were falling into a kind of routine. And so was our "music prep." We met after school every day except Friday. Our week was divided in half: two days of voice training and two days of choir practice. As we got closer to a performance, we were told, there'd be more practice and less training. That would suit me just fine.

The voice trainer turned out to be an older woman — about my great-grandmother's age — named Mrs. Wexler. She had a nice smile and rimless glasses that she wore perched at the edge of her long, thin nose. At our first lesson, she told me that I had a good voice but was using it all wrong.

"Wrong?" I repeated in shock. "How can I be using it wrong if the song comes out sounding nice?"

"It's wrong because it's making you strain your vocal cords," she explained. "If you do the exercises I show you, you'll be doing your vocal cords a favor. And the song will sound even better!"

I felt like saying that I was happy with my voice just the way it was. But then I thought about Chaya having *her* voice trained, and maybe shooting even further ahead of me than she already was. So I just nodded and said meekly, "Okay, Mrs. Wexler."

To my surprise, I didn't mind the voice lessons. The exercises were repetitive and kind of boring, but I liked the way they made my throat feel when I sang. I wasn't sure, but I thought I was starting to notice a difference.

Still, my favorite days of the week were the days our choir got together to practice. Knowing that there was a performance coming up gave our rehearsals an extra edge. It made the singing even more exciting — and it had been exciting enough to start with!

"This harmony is so complicated," a girl named Rochel complained that first Thursday. I was finding it complicated, too, though not enough to complain about.

"Good," Miss Sperling said. "That means it's not your usual, run-of-the-mill harmony. Complicated is interesting."

"But it's so hard to learn," Dina whined.

"Of course it is," Miss Sperling said briskly. "Anything

worthwhile is worth a little extra effort."

She looked around at the rest of us, her expression serious. "I'm talking to all of you, girls. Don't expect this choir to be a walk in the park. It's going to take work. *Hard* work — and lots of it. We aim high! We want everyone to know that the JAPA choir is a cut above."

Hearing that made us stand straighter. It made me feel as if every bit of the work would be worth it.

"But we have to work as a team," Miss Sperling continued. "Each one of you will shine as part of the choir. Only by working together will we put on the best performance that we possibly can!"

After that pep talk, nobody complained about the complicated harmonies anymore. We did our best to follow along, and when we messed up, we went back to the beginning and tried again.

"Not bad," Miss Sperling said, when the session was done. "We're going to have a broken practice schedule over the next couple of weeks because of the Yamim Tovim. After Succos, though — watch out! Then we're going to *really* start working!"

Scary words — but she said them with a smile.

I thought about what Miss Sperling had said about each of us getting to shine, and about making our choir a cut above the ordinary.

And that made me smile, too.

Chapter 18

The Apology

"Hi, Ora!" Penny greeted me the next day — the first Friday of the school year. "I just had a fantastic idea! Do you want to come over to my house tomorrow? Or is it too far to walk?"

My heart started doing handsprings. "I don't think it's too far. It shouldn't take me more than fifteen or twenty minutes," I said, trying to sound casual about it all. "No problem."

"Great! Come at about two, okay? I'll introduce you to whoever's around and we can spend the whole afternoon together!"

I didn't want to ask. I knew I shouldn't ask. But I *had* to ask. "Will Chaya be there, too?"

Penny looked surprised. "Actually, I was planning to invite her. Why not?"

I could have given her about fifty reasons why not, but they were not reasons that Penny would have appreciated. So I just bit my tongue and echoed, "Why not?"

All at once, half of my pleasure in the upcoming visit to Penny's house went up in smoke.

But there was still the other half. And that was enough to keep me going.

This was ridiculous. Here it was, Erev Shabbos already, and Bassi and I were still not speaking.

I didn't know how my sister felt, but it creeped me out. Imagine living in the same house — in the same *room* — as someone, and not exchanging a word with them. How crazy is that?

Like I said, Bassi isn't the kind of girl who gets mad often. In fact, I couldn't remember the last time she'd been this angry at me. But I didn't know how to end our fight.

I had a feeling that I was supposed to apologize, but what for? I'd only said the truth, right? Of course Bassi was jealous that she couldn't go to JAPA like me! Wouldn't anyone be?

"Okay, what's going on with you two?" Mommy asked. It was Friday afternoon, and we were both supposed to be helping her finish preparing for Shabbos. Not speaking to each other while crammed into the same kitchen was making the atmosphere very uncomfortable. So uncomfortable, that our mother picked up on it. Or had she already figured it out but was waiting to see what we would do on our own?

Whichever one it was, it looked like Mommy was finally fed up.

Bassi glanced at me and then looked away again. I looked at Mommy and said, "We, er, had a little fight."

"A *little* fight!" Bassi exploded. Then she clamped her lips together tight, as if she wanted to prevent another word from escaping.

"Do you want to tell me about it?" Mommy asked. "Or can the two of you work it out by yourselves?"

Neither one of us answered.

"I guess there's my answer," my mother sighed. "Well, what was the fight about?"

Bassi surprised me by offering an answer. "Ora seems to think that I must be *burning* with envy because she goes to JAPA and I don't. She didn't believe me when I said that I wasn't jealous at all!"

Mommy nodded her head slowly. Then she looked at me. "Ora? Is this true?"

"Is what true?" I asked cautiously.

"Is it true that you didn't believe what Bassi told you?"

I thought about how to answer that. "It's not that I thought she was lying, exactly," I said at last. "It's just that…"

"*What*?" Bassi snapped.

I shrugged. "You could be jealous and not even realize it. Unconsciously, know what I mean?"

My sister made her opinion of *that* very clear. She gave a loud sniff and turned her back on me.

Mommy said, "Ora, I think you owe your sister an apology. It's rude and hurtful to accuse someone of being jealous… and then accuse them of not even being *aware* that they're jealous. Don't you think?"

I shrugged again. "Whatever."

"Is that a yes or a no?"

Actually, it had been an *I-wish-we-weren't-having-this-conversation* kind of shrug. But Mommy was waiting for an answer, and I was sick and tired of this silent war with Bassi. So I said, "Yes, I guess it's rude and hurtful."

"And don't you think you should apologize?"

"Whatever. I'm sorry," I said to Bassi's back.

She whirled around. "That sounded *so* sincere," she said sarcastically.

"I said I'm sorry, okay? Can we just forget it?"

I saw my sister struggle. She was still mad at me, but she didn't want to be. If I hated this fight, my sister hated it even more.

And then I saw just why everyone always says that Bassi is one of the nicest people they know. The reason is that she *is* nice.

And because she's so nice, she put away her anger, gave me a sad little half-smile, and said, "Fine. Apology accepted. We'll forget it."

But even I, as dense as I can sometimes be, knew that neither one of us would really forget it. And the reason for that is because we never really resolved the fight. We just sort of pushed it under the rug so we could be comfortable again.

And we all know how well *that* works.

That night, I tried not to spend the whole Shabbos *seudah* talking about JAPA and my choir. But it was hard.

I had so much to say that I went on and on. This was

the first time in my life that I felt important and interesting, and I wasn't about to let this opportunity pass me by.

At one point, Abba took advantage of a brief lull to start singing *zemiros*. Then Mommy put me in charge of serving dessert and I had to go into the kitchen. Still a little nervous around Bassi, I gave her an extra-big portion. She smiled and thanked me.

But afterward, when we went upstairs, things were still awkward between us. I felt as if I had to measure every word before I said it — and I'm pretty sure that my sister felt the same way. The kind of thing they call "walking on eggshells." Would we ever be back to normal again?

But I was too tired to spend much time thinking about it. I slept deeply, and before I knew it, it was Shabbos morning. And then it was Shabbos afternoon, and time to get ready to go to Penny's house!

I spent an anxious half-hour standing at the big window in the living room and gazing up at the sky. It was overcast and cloudy. I pictured those clouds filled with millions of drops of water, all waiting to pour down on my head. I clenched my fists and closed my eyes. *Please don't rain, please don't rain, please don't rain…*

It didn't rain.

In fact, after a while the wind moved some of the clouds out of the way to let a pale bit of sunshine peek through.

"Bye, Ma! I'm going now!"

My mother, who'd been playing with Huvi and little Shmulie on the couch, looked up and smiled. "Good Shabbos, Ora. Have a nice time with your friends."

I fully intended to have a nice time… with the girl who

was actually *my friend*.

As for Penny's other guest — well, I wouldn't think about that now.

I stepped out into the street and turned right, walking fast. It was a quarter to two, the sun was almost shining, and Penny was waiting!

Chapter 19

Three's a Crowd

Penny's house was one of those big, rambling, sagging places that look as if it's a hundred years old. The kind of house where the paint is peeling and the wood on the front porch looks weathered. The kind of house that makes you feel instantly at home.

I knocked on the door, which was thrown open by a cute little red-haired boy. He had a button nose sprinkled with freckles and Penny's friendly smile.

"Good Shabbos," I said. "I'm a friend of Penny's. Is —"

The boy turned around and hollered, "PENNY! YOUR FRIEND IS HERE!"

While I waited for Penny, four or five other kids came over to stand next to the boy who'd opened the door. They were different ages, but all of them were pretty young. About half of them were flaming redheads. The other half had light-brown hair, but they all had Penny's hazel eyes. The eyes stared at me with frank curiosity.

"What's your name?" asked a little girl who didn't look more than three.

"Ora," I said with a smile. "What's yours?"

She lit up, happy to have a chance to show off what she knew. She took a deep breath and began to rattle off: "My name is Ellie Kellman, and I'm almost four years old, and I have a phone number." She proceeded to rattle the number off, too. "*And* I have an address!" That came next. She looked at me expectantly, waiting for me to applaud. Or maybe to show her what *I* knew.

I said, "Good job!" I was about to rattle off my phone number when Penny appeared at the head of the steps.

"Hi, Ora!" she called, coming down the stairs. She laughed at the herd of kids standing around watching me as if I were an exotic animal in the zoo. "Let me introduce you. This is Reuvy, who's ten, then Asher, eight, and Zevi, who's five."

Zevi was the doorman who'd let me in. He was also, I remembered, the one who'd tried to make his own kind of brownies and ended up painting the kitchen walls with chocolate.

"Pleased to meet you," I told the three boys.

"And my little sisters," Penny continued, pointing in turn at each of the little girls. "Ellie."

I grinned at the little girl. "We've met."

"Yael," Penny said, fluffing her little sister's bouncing curls. "And this cutie" — Penny scooped up a toddler who had a thumb in her mouth and a tiny ponytail of red curls at the very top of her head — "is the youngest Kellman of them all. Zahavi!"

"Hi, there," I said, with a smile all around.

Ellie fixed me with a wounded look. "Aren't you pleased to meet *us*, too?"

"Of course I am," I said, startled.

"Well, why didn't you say so?"

"Oh. Sorry! I'm absolutely *thrilled* to meet you. All of you."

"My father says that Ellie's got the personality of a lawyer," Penny told me with a grin. "She doesn't let anyone get away with anything."

"I'm going over to Yanky's house, okay?" Reuvy asked. He was already halfway to the door.

With her older sisters gone and her parents resting, Penny was in charge. "Fine," she said. As her brother left, she told me, "His friend Yanky lives just down the block."

I followed Penny into the kitchen. As soon as I walked in, I sneaked a look at the walls. To my disappointment, the chocolate "wallpaper" was gone. Penny took a pitcher of cold juice out of the fridge. She was just reaching for the paper cups when we heard a strange sound coming from the living room.

Hup… hup… hup… It sounded like a herd of elephants on parade.

Penny listened for a minute, frowning. "I'd better go see what's up," she said. She clearly took her job of being in charge seriously. She left the kitchen, with me on her heels, curious to see what was going on.

Zevi was leading Ellie, Yael, and Asher around the living room — but not only on the floor. After a short march across the room, they clambered onto the couch and were bouncing their way in a line across it. As we watched, Zevi jumped across from the couch to an armchair, and from there to another couch.

"C'mon!" he yelled, motioning vigorously to his siblings. "*March*, you guys! *Hup... hup... hup...*"

Asher, who was eight, followed his younger brother easily. Ellie managed to follow along pretty well, too. But little Yael was having a harder time. She was okay on the couch, but when it came to crossing the gap between the couch and the armchair, she just couldn't do it. Down she fell into the crack between them. She sat there, curled up like a wounded bird who'd fallen out of her nest, rubbing her bumped knee and whimpering.

Penny crossed the room and picked her up. "What're you doing, Zevi? And why aren't you doing it on the floor?"

"We're soldiers on a boat. I forget what it's called..."

"The navy?"

"Right!" Zevi's freckled face lit up. "We're navy soldiers —"

"I think the word you want is sailors, Zevi."

"Okay, we're sailors. I'm the captain and these are my men." He waved an arm toward Asher, Ellie, and the whimpering Yael.

"But why are you marching on the couches?" Penny asked.

"Soldiers *always* march. Everyone knows that," Zevi said scornfully.

Penny shook her head. "I'm not asking why you're marching. I'm asking why you're marching on the *couches*. Why not on the floor?"

Zevi looked at the floor, and then back at Penny. "That?" he asked incredulously. "That's the ocean! How can we march on the ocean?"

I saw Penny trying to decide if it was worthwhile arguing with him. I guess she decided it wasn't, because she sort of sighed and then said, "I'm glad to see you at least took off your shoes." A pile of them sat in a jumble in a corner of the living room.

With a last kiss for Yael, she put her little sister down and led the way back to the kitchen. As we went, I could hear the "*Hup... hup... hup*" start all over again.

"Where are your older sisters?" I asked.

"At their friends' houses. Maybe you'll meet them later." Penny pulled a family-sized package of chips, some pretzels, and an enormous bag of popcorn out of the pantry and plunked them down on the table along with the juice and cups. Then she sat down, picked up little Zahavi, and cuddled her in her lap.

"When is Chaya coming?" I asked. I wished that Penny would say, "Never."

"Pretty soon, I hope." Zahavi took her thumb out of her mouth long enough to eat a pretzel, and then popped it back in. Before long, she was dozing peacefully against Penny's chest.

The two of us poured ourselves drinks and helped ourselves to snacks. And then we sat and talked.

I was glad that Chaya wasn't there yet. Here was my chance to finally get to know Penny! We weren't surrounded by other kids like we were at school, and we didn't have to shout to be heard above the noise in the schoolyard.

I told her about my family, and what it was like to have a perfect older sister. Penny said that her big sisters were almost perfect, too, but she didn't really mind.

"Doesn't *anything* bother you?" I asked wistfully.

Penny laughed. "Sure. Lots of things!"

"Name one."

She thought for a minute. Then she grinned. "Having people ask me what bothers me!"

We both laughed. I felt my spirits rise even higher.

But not for long…

There was a knock on the door. And then Zevi, the doorman, bellowed, "PENNY! YOUR OTHER FRIEND IS HERE!"

Chapter 20

The Thundercloud

Zahavi had fallen fast asleep on Penny's lap. Carefully Penny stood up, holding an armful of slumbering baby sister. She put Zahavi down in her playpen and covered her with a blanket.

"I think we had some cookies…" She went back to the freezer and rummaged inside. "Yes!" She had just pulled out the package when Zevi poked his head back into the kitchen.

In one long, breathless sentence, he said: "Your-other-friend-is-here-and-can-I-have-a-cookie-too?"

"I heard you the first time, Zevi. Here's a cookie. Please don't make crumbs all over the place…" But Zevi had disappeared.

Penny followed her brother out of the kitchen — and came back again a second later with Chaya right behind her.

Chaya was followed by Penny's other brothers and

sisters, each of whom demanded a cookie, too. When all the cookies were distributed and the kids had scampered away to continue their game, Chaya gave me a shy smile and said, "Good Shabbos."

"Good Shabbos. That dress is stunning!" I might not want her around right now, but I was determined to be nice.

Chaya blushed. "Thanks. I like yours, too."

Penny and I moved over to make room for her at the table.

"How long did it take you to walk here?" Penny asked.

"About fifteen minutes," Chaya said.

"Same as me," I put in.

"Except that you both came from opposite directions. So I guess I'm the monkey in the middle." Penny giggled.

We munched and talked. I found out that Penny loved Navi but had a hard time with memorizing dates in history. Chaya confided, with a shudder, that she loathed math. I wondered why she was in the high math group with me if she hated it so much, but I didn't ask. Things were going pretty well, until the subject of the choir came up.

"How do you like choir so far?" Chaya asked me, with the same shy smile.

"I love it," I said. Out of nowhere, a black cloud descended on me. "But I bet *you* love it even more."

"Me? Why?"

"Because you're the star. Miss Sperling is crazy about your voice!"

Chaya's face turned the color of a ripe tomato. "She likes yours, too. She said it was powerful."

"One of you is a great alto and the other is a great

soprano," Penny said quickly. "This is not a competition, you know."

But she was wrong. It sure *felt* like a competition. At least to me...

I had switched to this school so I could have a chance to shine. A place where I could feel special. But who was really the shining star in our choir?

I had a feeling it was the girl sitting across from me at Penny's kitchen table.

I couldn't say any of this out loud, so I bit my lip and said nothing. Inside, though, that thundercloud grew bigger and my mood got blacker. Between Bassi at home and Chaya at school, would I *ever* get to be number one?

Probably not, I thought gloomily. It was just my lot in life. Second fiddle.

Feeling the way I did, it was hard to sit across from Chaya and make conversation. I had been determined to be nice, but it wasn't working very well. Logical or not, right then it felt like it was all *her* fault I was always second best. I felt she was taking things away from me that I wanted.

Like Penny. And the spotlight in choir...

To make myself feel better, I decided to simply pretend that Chaya wasn't there. If I had something to say, I said it to Penny. If Chaya said something, I acted as if I didn't hear.

Once or twice, I caught Penny giving me a puzzled look, but I ignored those, too. As the afternoon wore on we played a couple of games, helped Penny feed the baby, and then — about two hours after she'd arrived — Chaya said that she had to go home.

I could have gone home then, too. But I stayed right where I was.

Chaya walked home slowly, head down, eyes focused on her feet. She'd been so excited about coming to spend the afternoon with Penny and Ora. So happy.

Now… not so much.

Penny was fine, but for some reason, Ora didn't seem to like her. That hurt. But what hurt even more was not knowing the reason why!

Chaya was not what you'd call the life-of-the-party type. She was on the quiet side. She didn't have a ton of friends, but she was fiercely loyal to the ones she had. Now that she'd changed schools, she was in the market for some new friends. All of them were. She'd been thrilled when she and Penny started carpooling together. It was a tailor-made way to get acquainted.

But Penny had already made friends with Ora, and Ora seemed to have something against Chaya. Chaya just wished she knew what it was.

"Good Shabbos!" she called to her mother as she walked through her front door. It was hard not to compare her own big, stately home with Penny's rather ramshackle one. Everything here looked shiny and well-kept. Even the sign on the door, "Tannenbaum Family," gleamed invitingly.

On the other hand, Penny's house was filled with kids and noise and laughter. Chaya's was mostly filled with silence.

She found her mother seated on one of the couches in the living room, turning the pages of a magazine.

"Good Shabbos, Chaya," Ima said, with the special smile she reserved only for Chaya and her twin brother, Nachy. Ima and Abba had been married a long time before the twins were born. That made their children doubly precious to them. "How did you enjoy your afternoon with Penny and — who was the other girl?"

"Ora Weiss. She's in my class, too."

Mrs. Tannenbaum nodded. "Did you have a nice time?"

Chaya hesitated. She wanted to be honest, but she also hated to worry her mother.

"It was fine," she said at last. Because parts of it had been fine.

All the parts that didn't include Ora Weiss.

I was glad to have a little more time alone with Penny. Maybe we could pick up where we'd been before Chaya came.

But Penny was in a strange mood when she returned to the kitchen after seeing Chaya off. For the first time since I'd known her, the big smile was nowhere in sight. Her usually cheerful face looked troubled.

"Ora?"

"Hm?"

"What's wrong?" Penny asked.

"Wrong? What should be wrong?"

"You've been acting… weird… all afternoon."

Not all afternoon, I thought. Just since Chaya barged

in. Before that, everything was just dandy.

"Weird how?" I asked, pretending that I didn't understand.

"I dunno. You didn't say much. Especially to Chaya. You acted as if she were invisible or something."

I shrugged.

"What do you have against her, anyway?" Penny persisted. "She's a really nice girl."

"I have nothing against Chaya. I just... would have been happier if she wasn't here, that's all."

"But why?"

I shrugged. "I didn't choose her, Penny. She's *your* friend, not mine."

"But why can't we *all* be friends?" she wailed.

I knew the answer. We couldn't all be friends because I was jealous. I wanted to outshine Chaya in choir — and I wanted Penny to be *my* special friend.

In fact, my life would be pretty much perfect if only Chaya wasn't around...

Somehow, Penny seemed to figure this out. Slowly, she said, "This is not like an exclusive club. Know what I mean?"

"Who said anything about exclusive?" I put on an innocent face, as if I didn't know what she was talking about.

She shook her head. "All I know is that you get weird whenever Chaya's around. But she's a person, too. A nice person. And," she added with spirit, "a person who's a part of my life, just like you are. I hope you can accept that."

I didn't know if I could accept it or not. That must

have shown on my face, because Penny looked sad. And a little mad, too.

"Guess it's time to go," I said.

Penny walked me to the door. "Good Shabbos," I said. "See you at school."

"Yeah. See you." Her voice was stiff.

Penny stood by the door and watched me walk away. When I looked back over my shoulder, she flashed me a smile that looked forced. Her expression was still troubled.

When I got home and Mommy asked me how the visit had gone, I returned an automatic, "Fine."

Parts of it *had* been fine. Up until the moment Chaya had walked into Penny's kitchen, that was. After that, things had pretty much gone downhill...

It hadn't been Penny's fault. It hadn't even been Chaya's fault. Not really. It had all been my doing.

All because of the black thundercloud that had filled my heart and refused to go away.

Chapter 21

Binny in Trouble

Binny was excited.

It was Erev Succos and there was no school. He and his father had put up the succah days ago, and he'd promised to help his sisters decorate it later. But right now, he had more important business on his mind.

"Ma!" he shouted, bursting into the kitchen where his mother and sisters were busy cooking for Yom Tov. "Yitzi just called. He says some guys are coming over to play basketball in his yard. Can I go?"

His mother looked doubtful. "Aren't you supposed to be helping with the decorating?"

"Bassi and Ora aren't even ready yet. And anyway, I'll only be gone for, like an hour. Can I? Can I?"

Bassi took pity on her younger brother. "Mommy, we have plenty more to do here before we go out to decorate the succah."

"That's true." Mommy turned to Binny. "Okay, you can

go. But when you come back, I'll expect all hands on deck! No kvetching that you're too tired to decorate."

"No problem!" Smiling from ear to ear, Binny ran to the back door and disappeared.

He was in a tearing hurry. The problem with going to Yitzi's house was that Yitzi only let four kids at a time play with his basketball hoop — including himself, of course. He said that there wasn't enough room in the yard for more than that to play comfortably. If you were not among the first three boys to get there, you were forced to wait and watch. *Bo-ring!*

Yitzi didn't want to waste this precious hour watching other kids play ball. He wanted to get there as soon as humanly possible. He raced across his back yard and was about to start through to the yard next door when he stopped short. It was as if someone had pulled a string and yanked him back.

Since his father had told him to stay out of Mr. Grossbaum's yard, Binny had tried to remember. He would trudge obediently down his whole block, around the corner and down *that* block, until he reached Yitzi's house.

But all too often, by the time he got there, the yard was already full of kids who lived closer and had arrived before him. Most of the time, Binny never even got to play.

Not this time, he told himself. Today, he was going to finally get to shoot some hoops!

Or was he?

He stood uncertainly for a few seconds, fighting with himself. He wanted to respect Mr. Grossbaum's wishes.

But he also wanted to play in Yitzi's yard. He wanted it badly.

Just this once, he told himself, starting to move again. I'll cross Mr. Grossbaum's yard so carefully that I won't even come within a *mile* of his precious roses. He won't even know I was there...

The back yards of all the houses were like one long lawn stretching far down the block. Binny ran through them, one after another, keeping up a good pace. At this rate, he'd be among the first to reach Yitzi's house for sure! He put on an extra burst of speed anyway.

And then — he stopped short. The invisible string yanked him back a second time as he gaped in disbelief.

That tall fence had not been here the last time he'd come this way. But it sure was here now!

It was standing right in his way, between the Kleins' yard and Mr. Grossbaum's.

It was a simple wire fence, the kind you can see through. But it might as well have been made of solid brick. It seemed to be mocking Binny, telling him, "You thought you could cross this way? Well, think again..."

Binny drew in a long, moaning breath. He was winded from his run but, even more, he was filled with chagrin.

By the time he made his way back to the sidewalk and around the block to Yitzi's house, it would be too late. Once again, he'd have to stand and watch the other guys have fun without him. It just wasn't fair!

Balefully, he glared at the fence. He didn't know when Mr. Grossbaum had put it up, because he hadn't come this way in a while. But it couldn't have been too long ago. On the other side were Mr. Grossbaum's flowerbeds and then more lawn… stretching all the way down to the Feinblums' house, where there was a shortcut leading straight to Yitzi's back yard.

He pictured the other kids there, happily bouncing the basketball and shooting it up in the air. He pictured the ball dropping neatly into the hoop. Binny wasn't so good at getting it to go through the hoop yet. But he *would* be, if only he had a little more practice!

At this rate, it looked like he'd *never* get to practice with Yitzi's hoop. And, even more than that, he wanted to be part of Yitzi's crowd. But how could *that* happen if he always came late?

Suddenly, he had an idea.

He looked up at the fence again. It was tall — but not *too* tall. There was no barbed wire on top or anything like that, just tips of twisted metal where the strands of wire met. The holes in the fence weren't big, but he thought they were big enough for his sneakered feet to fit inside.

Without stopping to think, he bounded forward, gripped the fence with both hands, and stuck his foot in one of the holes formed by the strands of meshed wire.

It fit!

Elated, he found another toehold.

Inch by inch, he hauled himself up. The fence swayed alarmingly with his weight, but it held. Another foot higher… and then another. He had reached the top!

Here came the really tricky part.

He had to find a way over the twisted tips of metal so that he could start down the other side. Carefully, he lifted one leg and, holding on for dear life, put it over the top of the fence. He was about to do the same thing with his other leg when a sound made him freeze.

It was the sound of a window opening. A window nearby.

Was it Mr. Grossbaum?

Binny didn't wait to find out. With a gasp, he tried to finish wriggling over to the other side of the fence so he could drop down to the ground and run for his life. In his haste, however, all he managed to do was snag a piece of his polo shirt on one of the metal tips sticking out on top.

"Miri! Time to come inside!"

It wasn't Mr. Grossbaum at the window after all. It was a different neighbor who'd thrown open the window — some mother calling her little girl home. But that didn't help Binny's predicament. His shirt was still tangled in the wire.

Gritting his teeth, he tried to pull the material free. That just tangled it worse.

Finally, in desperation, he gave the hem of his shirt an enormous yank... and heard the fabric rip loose.

Unfortunately, that yank made him lose his balance. Binny started sliding back down the fence. He grabbed frantically at the mesh wire to break his fall, and managed to slow himself enough so that he landed with a small thud instead of a huge one.

But he was shaken all over. Every bone ached.

He looked down at himself. His shirt was ripped, but that wasn't the worst of the damage. When he'd fallen, he had landed on a pointy rock and scraped himself. He stared at the long gash, oozing blood down the middle of his forearm.

He hadn't even felt it at the time... but he felt it now. Oh, how he felt it. Tears of pain sprang into his eyes as the scrape began to sting.

He pulled himself slowly to his feet, feeling his bones ache where he'd fallen on them. He looked back over his shoulder and thought gloomily, "Well, if I had to fall, at least it wasn't on Mr. Grossbaum's precious flowers!"

And then he started trudging back the way he'd come. It was time to go home and take care of this cut before it bled all over the place.

He used the bottom of his shirt to catch the worst of the blood drips as he made his way to his house. When he reached the back door, he paused.

He didn't want to go through the kitchen, because his mother would take one look at him and the whole story would come out. All about his decision to cut through the back lawns *just this once...* about Mr. Grossbaum's new fence... about Binny's attempt to climb... and about his fall.

He decided to take his chances with the front door.

Opening it cautiously, he stuck his head inside and looked around. The coast was clear. From the kitchen came the voices of his mother and sisters. Huvi had gone with their father to do some last-minute shopping, and Shmulie was probably still down for a nap. Binny tiptoed to the stairs and started climbing.

Every step seemed to take more effort than it should. It was as if his body was finally reacting to the shock of his fall. Everything hurt. His arm was still bleeding. He reached the head of the stairs and slipped gratefully into the bathroom, unseen...

Or so he thought.

Chapter 22
Ora to the Rescue

I was done in the kitchen. Bassi was still finishing up a recipe, but Mommy said I could go. I'd just stepped out of the kitchen when, out of the corner of my eye, I saw something move.

Whatever it had been was somewhere above my head. Looking up, I just managed to catch sight of my brother Binny as he climbed the last two steps to the landing. Then he practically ran into the bathroom and closed the door firmly behind him.

This was strange. Hadn't he just asked Mommy for permission to go to his friend's house? I'd seen him leave the house myself.

And there had been something odd in the way Binny had moved. As if something hurt him…

Puzzled, and a little scared, I hurried up the stairs after him.

"Binny?" I whispered into the door. I don't know why

I whispered. Maybe it was because of something else I'd picked up watching my brother go upstairs. He'd been half crouched over as if to make himself look smaller. Binny didn't want to be seen.

What was going on? Had my brother had an accident? Was he hurt? More urgently now, I tapped on the door and hissed, "Binny! Open up! It's me — Ora."

The door opened a crack. "Ora? Are you alone?" His whisper was hoarse.

"Yes. Are you okay?"

"Um… not so much."

"Let me in!"

There's nothing like seeing a younger sibling in pain to bring out all the big-sisterly feelings inside of you. I know that's how I felt when I saw the ugly scrape on my brother's forearm.

"Binny! How did you get that?"

He looked down at the scrape, too. He'd been trying to soak up the oozing blood with tissues but had just made a mess of things.

"I fell," he said.

"Fell where?"

He hesitated. "Promise you won't tell?"

"Tell what?" I asked impatiently. "Tell who?"

"Promise that you won't tell anyone what I'm going to tell you."

"Okay, okay," I said. "What is it?"

"I fell off Mr. Grossbaum's fence."

I blinked at him. "I didn't know he *had* a fence."

"Neither did I," Binny said with a sigh. "He must've just put it up."

"Why were you climbing his fence?"

"Because I wanted to get to Yitzi's house faster. So I could get to play."

Shaking my head, I said, "Didn't Abba tell you not to go that way?"

"I know. But I really wanted to get there fast. Just this once…"

I held up a finger. Then I cracked open the door and listened. Everything was quiet. Mommy and Bassi were still down in the kitchen and Shmulie was in his crib, napping. I closed the door again and turned back to my brother.

"Let me have a look at that," I said, gesturing at his arm. I'm a little nervous around blood, though not as nervous as some girls I know. Binny held out his arm and I inspected the scrape.

"It looks clean. That's good. What did you scrape it on?" It was actually a pretty superficial cut and hardly even bleeding anymore.

"A rock," Binny said. "When I fell off the fence."

"Okay. Let me clean you up."

Binny held out his arm and tried not to wince as I washed off the scraped place and then poured on some stinging stuff to kill the germs. After that, I found a ball of bandage and started winding it around his arm. The scrape, while not deep, was too long for a Band-Aid, or even a handful of them.

"Whew!" he said, when I was done. "I'm glad that's over with."

"Make sure you keep it clean," I told him.

"I will. But please don't tell Mommy or Abba. They'll

be mad at me for climbing Mr. Grossbaum's fence."

I wasn't sure what to do. *Baruch Hashem*, Binny wasn't hurt badly. But he *had* done something sort of dangerous. Was I obligated to tell my parents?

Binny gazed at me with pleading eyes and said, "I won't go that way ever again — I promise." Then he took away some of the power of that promise by adding, "I can't anyway. Because of the fence."

"Well, make sure you keep it clean," I said. "If it starts looking worse, I want you to tell Mommy right away."

"Okay."

I pierced him with my eyes. "I mean it, Binny. I'm going to check that wound myself. Every day. To make sure it's healing properly."

"It's not a wound! Just a little scrape."

"It's a *big* scrape," I corrected him.

"Okay, a big scrape," he conceded. "But still. You won't tell?"

"Not unless I have to," I told him.

And then Bassi was calling up the stairs, "Ora, do you want to get started on the succah before Binny gets home?"

"Okay," I called back. "Is Mommy still in the kitchen?"

"No, she went to the basement to do a last load of laundry before Yom Tov. Do you want me to call her?"

"No, that's okay…"

I put my mouth near Binny's ear and whispered, "I'll keep Bassi busy in the succah. Mommy's down in the laundry room. You can sneak out the back door and come back a little later through the front door. No one will know you were even home."

"Okay," he said, with a grateful nod. "Thanks, Ora."

"Don't mention it. But don't —"

"Do it again. I know."

With that, Binny held the door open for me to go out, and then closed it behind me.

As I went downstairs, there was a movie in my head of my brother climbing that fence and then falling down. The movie played over and over. Each time I heard the sound he made when he fell, my heart gave a little jolt. I hoped this whole thing wouldn't give me bad dreams tonight.

"Ora, are you okay? You've got a kind of funny look on your face."

Bassi was standing at the foot of the stairs, smiling at me quizzically. Her arms were loaded down with decorations.

I shook away the movie in my head. "I'm fine. Do you have the posters and streamers and everything?"

"Everything except the stuff that Huvi made in nursery school. She wants us to hang it in the succah. It's in her room. Can you get it?"

"Will do. Meet you in the succah in a minute."

I watched my sister leave and then ran back up the stairs. I tapped on the bathroom door and whispered, "The coast is clear. Go out the front door."

Binny whispered back, "Okay. Thanks!"

When I first saw him, bleeding in the bathroom, he looked pale and shaken and didn't sound much better. Now he sounded fine again. Just like his old self. I was glad.

We went our separate ways, Binny downstairs and me

to Huvi's room and then out to the succah. About twenty minutes later, Binny came in through the front door and hollered — loud enough for me to hear in the back yard — "I'm back! Who's ready to decorate?"

"Your sisters started without you," I heard Mommy tell him with a smile. "Go ahead and catch up."

Binny ran outside and joined us in the succah, which was already half-decorated.

"Hi, Binny. Can you push the ladder over this way?" I asked. I noticed that he was wearing a long-sleeved shirt now. He must have made a quick stop in his room to change before making his getaway.

"For you," my brother said, with a broad grin, "anything!"

Behind Bassi's back, he punctuated his answer with a wink.

Chapter 23

Ora Is Gracious

Anytime I had a spare minute, I did my voice exercises. Mrs. Wexler had said that we would notice a real difference if we kept up the exercises, and I wanted to have the very best voice that I possibly could. Especially with Chaya as my competition…

I was standing in my room, practicing my scales with my back to the door, when I heard, "What's that you're singing?"

You know the feeling you get when you think you're alone and then suddenly discover that you're not? I jumped six inches in the air!

When I landed on solid earth again, I turned around. There was Bassi, grinning at me. "Oops — sorry!" she said cheerfully. "I didn't mean to scare you."

My answer was a scowl. My heart was still thumping so hard I didn't know if I could say a word.

"Anyway," Bassi said, plopping down on her bed.

"What was it?"

"What was what?" I asked rudely.

"The song you were singing."

"That wasn't a song," I said loftily. "For your information, it was a scale. I was doing a voice exercise."

"Oh." Bassi tilted her head as though thinking it over, and then asked, "What's it supposed to do for your voice?"

"Make it better, of course."

"What, your voice isn't perfect already?" she teased.

I knew she was just kidding around with me. I knew that I should treat the comment as the joke that it was meant to be.

But all I could hear was the way she'd just poked fun at *the one thing* that I was better at than her. The one place where I did not have to play second fiddle.

"It's good enough," I said shortly. "But it could be better."

And then I walked right past my befuddled sister, and out the door.

On the second day of Succos, I had a surprise.

It was a warm, sunny afternoon, and I was up in my room relaxing with a book when I heard Mommy call up the stairs, "Ora! Your friends are here!"

Friends?

My first thought was Penny. But my mother had said "friends." Penny and Chaya?

Or maybe two other girls in my class had decided to pay a visit. Esti, or Fraidy — or Layala, maybe? They rode the van with me to and from school.

Devori and Ruthie were in choir with me, though so far we hadn't talked much. Could it be them?

I didn't know who had come visiting, but I was very glad they'd come.

Quickly, I pulled on a headband to hold back my unruly hair, which always seems to have a life of its own. Then I went out the door and almost flew down the stairs.

At the foot of the steps, I stopped short. I didn't see my visitors, but I sure recognized the voices I heard coming from the kitchen, where my sister was giving them a cold drink after their walk.

I knew what I was hearing, but I couldn't believe it.

I barged into the kitchen. "Shoshie? *Lana*?"

Lana was wearing a new Yom Tov outfit that I'd never seen before. Shoshie was wearing her hair in a different style than she had last year. In one way they were so familiar, but in another way, they seemed like strangers. I stared from one to the other, incredulous. They were the last two girls I'd expected to see!

Lana grinned at me smugly, thrilled that she'd managed to catch me by surprise.

"We were doing some succah-hopping," she said, "and we thought we'd hop over and see how you're doing."

"I'm doing fine," I croaked. My throat had suddenly gone dry.

It's funny, but even now that I was in a different school, I could still remember how it had felt to be with these two girls. How impatient Lana had been with me sometimes, and how bored I'd felt with their conversation.

Still, they had taken the trouble to come visit. It was

up to me to be a gracious hostess.

"Come see the succah," I invited, when they'd finished their drinks.

Lana and Shoshie trailed after me through the back door and into the succah. They spent a few minutes politely admiring the decorations, and then we sat down and looked at each other.

"So!" Lana said brightly. "How's your new school?"

She was, I saw, really curious. And why not? I'd be curious, too, if I were in her shoes.

"It… is… *fantabulous*," I said, stretching out the words to emphasize the point.

"Really?" Lana looked almost disappointed. As if she wouldn't have minded hearing that I was miserable. That I regretted switching schools.

"Really," I said firmly.

"What's so great about it?" Shoshie asked.

I didn't know where to begin.

"Well, we have an adorable building. And a great principal," I said. Should I have put the principal first? "The teachers are good, and I like the girls in my class."

I didn't tell them about Mrs. Mammon's speech at our opening assembly, where she said we would be like stars spilling our light onto the world. Somehow, that didn't feel like the right thing to say to outsiders. It had been meant just for us, the students in Mrs. Mammon's special new school.

"What about the performing arts part?" Lana asked, trying not to sound too eager but giving herself away by the eager gleam in her eye.

"I'm in the choir. There are twelve of us, plus another twelve in the dance group and eight in the band... I mean, the orchestra. Miss Sperling — that's our choir leader — says that they're looking for a couple more girls to round that out."

"How often are you going to perform? And where?" Lana asked.

"We're having our first performance on Chanukah, *im yirtzeh Hashem*," I told them. "Just for family members — plus a few women from different cities who might be interested in having us perform at their events. If they do end up booking us, we'll be traveling all over the place."

The two girls looked suitably impressed. I added proudly, "Miss Sperling says that the choir is the backbone of the whole program."

"Why?" Shoshie asked.

"Well, not every banquet or dinner will have room for a whole dance group to perform. And setting up an orchestra and their instruments needs room, too. But Miss Sperling says there's always enough space for a choir. So we'll probably get to perform the most often." I was zinging with pride as I said those words. I watched my guests' faces to see their reactions.

Lana's reaction was everything I could have wished for. Her eyes were wide with admiration — and something else.

The "something else" was envy. I recognized the envy because it had been my own closest companion for such a long time...

Shoshie leaned forward and asked, "Are the girls as good as they say?"

"Which girls?"

"All the girls in your school. They say only the best of the best were accepted. The best singers, dancers, and musicians."

I glowed with satisfaction. With pretend humbleness, I said, "I don't know about that… but the girls *are* awfully good."

"Including you?" Lana asked, with a trace of her old snideness.

I bowed my head modestly and didn't answer.

Lana and Shoshie couldn't get enough of my descriptions of JAPA — which suited me fine, since I loved to talk about it. I was in the middle of describing the stunning song we were learning for our first performance, when Bassi poked her head into the succah.

"Anyone interested in some cookies and lemonade?"

We were all interested. We accepted the pitcher and the loaded plate with a chorus of thanks. After Bassi went back into the house, Lana said around a mouthful of cookie, "Your sister is the best!"

I waited to feel the usual pang. Usually, any praise of Bassi made me feel bad because I thought that the person doing the praising was comparing my perfect sister to imperfect me. I knew that it should have been *me* who thought of bringing out something for my guests to eat and drink in the succah. And I would have, if I hadn't been so busy boasting about my school.

But the pang didn't come. A little thing like forgetting to offer my guests refreshments seemed — paltry. After an hour of pouring my stories into their ears and seeing the admiration in their eyes, I was all puffed up with how important I was. Compared to that, Lana and Shoshie were just ordinary, run-of-the-mill girls. Unlike me.

As Shayna liked to sing in the schoolyard every day, I was *sooo* special!

Nothing — not even yet another compliment for my sister, who seemed to rack them up by the dozens — could take that away from me.

Chapter 24

Chol HaMoed Blues

Bassi was in the kitchen when I came in after saying good-bye to my guests. "Had a nice visit?" my sister asked. She sounded okay, but she was avoiding my eyes.

"Uh-huh. It was fine. Thanks for the cookies and lemonade, by the way."

"You're welcome." Yes, Bassi was definitely acting weird. She looked as if she'd swallowed something and it was stuck in her throat.

I looked at her curiously. "What?"

Bassi hesitated.

"*What*?" I asked again.

"I don't know if I should say anything," she began. "I mean, it's not really any of my business."

I was about to suggest, "Then *don't*," when she continued, "Then again, I'm your sister. So maybe it *is* my business..."

"Bassi!" I yelped. "Would you just tell me already?"

At long last, she met my eyes. "I overheard what you were saying when I brought the stuff out to the succah. And it sounded a little…"

"A little *what*?"

"A little… show-offy."

I stared at her, hearing her words echo in my head. I didn't know what to think. Wouldn't *she* show off, too, if she'd been accepted by a school like JAPA and finally had a chance to lord it over a couple of girls from her old school who had always lorded it over *her*?

Then I answered my own question: Honestly? The answer was no. Bassi would *not* show off. She just wasn't made that way.

But it looked like I was.

I tossed my head as if to say, *So what*? "Thanks for the feedback," I said airily. "I'll take it under advisement." I'd heard that expression somewhere and had been waiting for a chance to use it.

"Ora —" Bassi looked troubled.

"Don't worry about whether you might have hurt my feelings," I said, in the same light-hearted tone. "Because you didn't."

With that, I walked airily out of the kitchen.

I headed straight for my room, and the book I'd left face-down on my bed when Lana and Shoshie came.

Reading is the best thing I know for keeping you from thinking about stuff you don't want to think about.

In our family, the first day of Chol HaMoed often slips by with nothing much happening. We're usually content just to hang around the house and make plans for the next day or two. Which was exactly what we were doing now.

"So, you're all up for Amazing Adventure Park tomorrow?" Abba asked.

We were sprawled around the living room, where we'd each been doing our own thing until my father spoke up. Abba had a *sefer* open in front of him, Mommy was leafing through the enormous Succos edition of her favorite magazine. Bassi and I were reading, and Binny was practicing his technique with some marbles on the floor while Huvi and Shmulie played nearby with some blocks.

"Yes!" we shouted. Or at least, some of us did. It seemed we were all up for the trip... except Bassi.

"Actually," my sister said, "I'm not that crazy about amusement parks. Would you mind if I do something with my friends instead?"

"Won't they be going somewhere with their families?" Mommy asked.

"At least two of them are planning to stay home because their families are going somewhere they don't like. So I thought I'd hang out with them. Is that okay?"

My mother frowned. She really likes when our whole family does things together. She says that having adventures together makes memories. But this particular adventure didn't appeal to Bassi, so my parents — while they would miss her — agreed to let her do her own thing.

"That means there'll be an extra seat in the van," Abba

remarked. "Anyone want to bring a friend?"

My "I do!" came so fast that no one else had a chance to answer. "I'll go call Penny right now!" I scrambled to my feet.

Luckily for me, Penny was home, though she told me that her parents were taking the whole family out for a picnic a little later. "What's up?" she asked.

"We're going to Amazing Adventure Park tomorrow — and we have an extra seat! Want to come?"

I'd expected either an excited, "Yes!" or a regretful, "Sorry, I can't make it." What I didn't expect was a long silence.

"Penny?" I asked. "You still there?"

"I'm here," she said. "Just thinking…"

"Well, can you come, or can't you?"

"I don't think I can make it," she said slowly. I'd have expected to hear regret in her voice — but I heard something else. I wasn't sure what it was, but I didn't think I liked it.

"Oh, that's too bad. Sure you can't switch things around so you can join us? We'll have a blast!"

"Actually, my own family's been thinking about going to the same amusement park," Penny said.

"Would you be going tomorrow or the next day?"

"I'm not sure."

"Well, if you can't come with us, maybe I'll see you there tomorrow," I said hopefully. "We could go on some rides together."

"Maybe," she said. But she said it in a way that meant "probably not."

I hung up the phone, disappointed. But my spirits soon

lifted. It was Chol HaMoed, and we were getting ready to do fun stuff, and after that came Shemini Atzeres and Simchas Torah. Picturing little Shmulie's excitement when Abba picked him up and put him up on his shoulders for the *hakafos*, I had to smile.

And when all of that excitement was over, it would be back to JAPA and my amazing new life.

I couldn't wait!

"Yocheved?" Penny tapped on her oldest sister's bedroom door. "Can I come in?"

Yocheved had her own room, though it was not much bigger than a closet. When she called out, "Sure!" Penny opened the door and took one step into the room, which was about all you *could* take without bumping into something. Yocheved was propped up on a bunch of pillows on her bed next to the window, reading.

"Can I ask you something?" Penny asked, perching at the foot of her sister's bed.

Yocheved put aside her book. "Shoot."

"Well… I have this friend. Ora?"

"Yes, you told us about her. Still haven't met her, though."

"And I have this other friend," Penny went on. "Chaya."

"That's the pretty one, right? With the gorgeous voice?"

Penny nodded. "That's right."

"What about them?"

Penny settled herself more comfortably on the bed. From where she was sitting, she could see herself in the mirror on the back of her sister's closet. Her usually smiling face wore a perturbed look.

"I'm good friends with Ora," Penny said. "We first met in camp — just at the very end — and then we met up again in school. I really like her."

"So what's the problem?"

"The problem," Penny said with a sigh, "is that I like Chaya, too. But Ora doesn't!"

"Why not?" Yocheved asked in surprise.

Penny shrugged. "I don't have a clue. She just doesn't. The only time I had them both here together, it was awful. Ora basically acted as if Chaya didn't exist."

"Poor Chaya," Yocheved said, absently fingering the tassel on her window shade.

"I know," Penny agreed. She heaved a sigh. "You know that trip to Amazing Adventure Park we're supposed to be having this Chol HaMoed?"

"I'm not going," Yocheved reminded her. "Or Miriam." Miriam was the second-oldest sister in the family. Like Ora's sister Bassi, they had little interest in having their insides turned inside-out on roller coasters and Tilt-a-Whirls.

"I know," Penny said again. "So we have two extra seats in our van, and Ma said I could invite two friends to come with us if I want. But I can't invite both Ora and Chaya. I just can't! It'll just be a cold war between the two of them all over again. It'll be awful!"

Yocheved nodded slowly. "I see what you mean. No one'll end up having much fun."

"And now Ora just invited me to come with *her* family!"

Yocheved's eyes grew large. "The plot thickens," she murmured.

Penny nodded. "Anyway, I told Ora that I couldn't go with her because our family's planning to go. But I didn't invite her to join us — *or* tell her that I'm planning to invite Chaya. Was that wrong of me? Should I just invite no one?"

Her big sister thought about that for a long time. Finally, she shook her head and said, "I think this is on Ora. You can't have a war — cold or otherwise — unless at least one person wants it. And it's only Ora who seems to want it. So why should Chaya suffer?"

"That's what I thought." Penny clenched her fists. "I just wish they could both be friends. I wish…"

"If wishes were coins, we would all be as wealthy as kings," Yocheved quoted.

Penny looked up at her with miserable eyes. "You know what would make *me* feel rich? Having two friends who actually like each other!"

She thanked her sister for listening and left the room. She would call Chaya right away and issue her invitation.

She knew that it was the right thing to do. And she would have fun with Chaya, no question about that.

But how she wished that Ora — a happy, accepting, *friendly* Ora — could have been there, too!

Then her gloom turned into determination. She remembered how Ora had treated Chaya on Shabbos. What Ora was getting now was exactly what she deserved. It was nobody's fault but her own.

Penny marched over to the phone to call Chaya.

Chapter 25

Back to School

"You're looking happy today," Mommy said as I walked into the kitchen.

"I *am* happy!" There was a patch of sunlight right in the middle of the kitchen floor and I went to it and twirled around, a huge smile on my face.

Binny looked up from his cereal box — he was trying to figure out another puzzle — and asked, "Why?"

"Why not?" I asked, twirling again, and then a third time for good measure.

"I dunno. You're usually pretty grumpy."

Instantly, some of my good mood vanished. "I am not!"

"Sure you are," my brother said. "Everyone knows that."

"Well, *I* don't." I looked at my mother for confirmation, but all she did was give me a loving smile and murmur, "M is for 'moody,' remember?"

Yeah, I remembered. I stepped away from the sunshine

to take a seat at the table. "Well, I'm not being moody now. I'm being happy. There's a difference."

"Happy about what?" Bassi asked, walking in.

"I'm just glad to be going back to school today. Is that a crime?"

"It's no crime," Mommy said. "In fact — it's great! But you'd better eat your breakfast, or you'll be late for the van."

I reached for a bowl.

And approximately one hour later, I was in the parking lot of my lovely new school, looking around.

On every side, girls were emerging from big vans and private cars. The weather was unusually warm for an October morning, with scraps of high white clouds floating in a pale-blue sea. After the long Succos break, it felt like the start of the year all over again. Everyone was wearing that first-day-of-school look. Happy. Hopeful.

And mine was the happiest and most hopeful of them all!

A burst of laughter behind me made me turn around. It was Shayna again, entertaining her fellow ninth graders with her *"We're so special"* song. It reminded me of the way I'd entertained Lana and Shoshie in my succah the week before. Doing my best to make sure they knew just how special JAPA was. And how special *I* was!

I looked around for Penny, hoping for a few minutes before the bell rang so we could compare notes about Yom Tov.

A last car pulled up, and there was Penny.

Unfortunately, there was Chaya, too. They were together, as usual, and laughing about something when I came up to them.

"What's the joke?" I asked, trying not to feel left out but not succeeding very well.

Chaya started to answer, but Penny broke in — a little too hastily, it seemed to me. "Oh, nothing special," she said. She flashed me her sparkly smile. "What's doing, Ora? How was the rest of your Yom Tov?"

I would have been more than happy to tell her, but I didn't have the time. Before I'd finished my first sentence, the bell rang to usher us inside.

We crowded through the doors and piled into our classrooms.

That day, all our teachers made a point of reminding us that the break was over. The school year was about to begin in earnest now — and we were going to be given a heavy workload to prove it. There were moans and groans all around as we contemplated the heap of tests and assignments coming up.

But the biggest buzz came at recess. With Succos behind us, all everyone could talk about was Chanukah — and our very first performance of the year!

The show would take place in our own auditorium, and mostly for our own families. But rumors spread about who else had been invited. Heads of women's *tzedakah* organizations from far and wide. Women who held big events each year to raise money for their causes — and who just might want *us* to help them do it!

The day passed eventually, as even the longest school days do. We finally had our chance to talk after our last class, in the ten precious minutes before music prep began.

"C'mon," I urged. "Let's go down to the basement and

do some catching up!"

It wouldn't be long before I would be wishing that the chance had never come...

We were sitting in our usual spot, just outside the janitor's closet. Hearing the thumps and bumps coming from inside, Penny tapped on the door and called, "Hi, Gali! It's us!"

The door opened, and Gali appeared, face flushed and hair flying. She managed not to fall out the door this time.

"Hi, guys!" she said. "Am I bothering you?"

"Nope," I said.

Penny added, "Maybe we're bothering *you?*"

"No way," Gali said cheerfully. "In fact, I think I'll keep the door open, so I can hear you guys talk while I stretch. It's much less boring that way!"

Did I mention that Chaya was with us, too? If I didn't, it's because I was doing my usual thing of making believe she wasn't there. I would much rather have had Penny to myself, but Chaya seemed glued to her like a shadow these days — and not only during their carpool.

"Talk, Ora," Penny prompted as we took our places with our backs to the wall — Penny in the middle, with Chaya and I flanking her on both sides and Gali listening in from the closet. "What did you do on Chol HaMoed and the rest of Yom Tov?"

I told them about our Chol HaMoed trips, and about an interesting new dessert that I'd helped my mother make for one of the meals. The cake had flopped instead of rising, but turned out to be delicious anyway. Then I described Simchas Torah, especially the dramatic mo-

"Fun," I repeated. My head bobbed up and down like a broken puppet. Or a robot.

"Chaya's parents weren't planning to take her and her brother this year," Penny explained, still giving me that same uneasy look. "And I knew that *you* were going anyway, with your family. So…"

"So," I said, even more robotlike.

"So." Penny sighed.

Chaya looked at both of us, wondering what was going on.

And then Gali popped out of the closet like a Jack-in-the-Box to ask breathlessly, "Are any of you wearing a watch? I think it's time —"

She was interrupted by Mrs. Reingold's voice over the intercom, telling us that it was time to head to our music prep rooms.

We climbed the stairs to the lobby, where Gali split off to go to the auditorium for her dance practice. Chaya started down the hall to Room 8, and I was about to follow when Penny grabbed my arm. I turned my head to look at her. Her expression was agonized.

"Wait a second, okay?" she whispered. "I need to tell you something!"

Chapter 26
Strike Two

"I just want to explain," Penny said, talking fast.

There were not many girls left in the lobby now. Everyone had gone to their music prep room to rehearse. We needed to get moving, too.

"Explain what?" I asked coldly. The first shock had started to dribble away, but my insides felt just as frozen as before.

"I wish we could have all gone together!" she burst out. "If only you…"

"If only I what?"

"If only you wouldn't make it so *hard*!"

I stared at Penny. Her big, sparkly smile was nowhere in sight. She looked frustrated, and angry, and perilously close to tears.

Before I could ask what she meant, she went ahead and told me.

"Why can't you be nicer to Chaya? I know that you're

a good person. But whenever you see her..." She shook her head. "You become someone else."

"Someone else?" I repeated, trying to pull my wits together. It was strange to see the usually super-cheerful Penny looking so devastated. It threw me off my balance and made it hard to think.

"Yes," she said. She looked down at the floor. "You stop being someone nice and become... someone mean."

I could feel myself flushing a deep, dark red. The color of bricks. "Oh, yeah?" I shot back. "Well, *you* stop being nice, too."

"When?" Penny asked, taken aback.

"When you basically dump one friend just because you found another one."

"What? I didn't dump —"

"Girls? Aren't you supposed to be somewhere?" It was Mrs. Reingold, the school secretary, giving us a disapproving look from the office doorway.

"Uh, right." Penny started down the hall toward Room 6, where the band — sorry, the *orchestra* — met. I trailed behind her. Just before she went inside, she looked back over her shoulder and gave me a kind of despairing look. I pretended not to see it and continued down the hall until I reached Room 8.

When I walked in, Miss Sperling was checking her watch and saying, "Does anyone know where Ora is?"

"I'm right here," I volunteered, trying to shake off the effects of Penny's words. And the shock of finding out that Penny had invited Chaya to go to the amusement park with her instead of coming with me and my family. Or inviting me to come with her...

Miss Sperling frowned. "You're late, Ora. Music prep started five minutes ago." She clasped her hands together and swept the whole choir with her eyes. "We're a team, remember? And every member of a team depends on everyone else to be punctual and get the job done. Right?"

I nodded dumbly. Right.

"Okay. Positions, please."

We scurried over to our allotted places — sopranos on the right and altos on the left. I noticed Chaya peeking over at me, but I pretended not to see. When we were settled, Miss Sperling took her place in front and said, "It's exactly two months to Chanukah, girls. We have a lot of work to do to get ready for our performance. Let's see what you remember from before Succos... Okay, the song I was in the middle of teaching you. Take it from the top!"

We opened our mouths and began to sing.

The words and melody filled the room with lovely sound. While I was singing, nothing could bother me. Not Penny's outburst, not my own insecurities, not even Chaya singing her heart out on the other side of the room. For a few minutes, there was nothing but the music, and using my voice to make it as beautiful as it could be.

"Not bad," Miss Sperling said when we were done. Then she proceeded to pick the song apart. This note had to be slightly stronger, that note slightly lower, and a third note didn't belong there at all. She had the high voices go over their part, and then the low ones. Then she told us to put it all together again.

"Better," she commented. "Of course, it's going to sound much more professional once you have a few weeks of voice training under your belts."

"What's the point of that?" someone asked. I was pretty sure her name was Dina. An eighth grader.

"The point of training your voices?"

Dina nodded. I noticed a few other girls nodding, too.

"There are a few reasons," Miss Sperling said. "The vocal cords are made of muscle, just like the other muscles in your body. When you train and exercise them, your range will increase. That means that you'll be able to reach notes that are higher and lower than you ever managed to reach before."

"Cool!" someone called out.

"Yes, it is. Not only that, but training helps your stamina, too. It gives your voice more strength, and helps prevent you from straining your voice, or even losing it entirely."

"Like laryngitis?" Dina asked.

"Something like that. We want to take care of our voices, girls, and use them like the amazing instruments Hashem intended them to be!"

If the rehearsal had stopped there, I would have been fine. But it didn't stop there. We still had another ten minutes to go, and Miss Sperling decided to use them to start figuring out the solos.

"There are three places where I think a solo or a duet would work nicely," she told us. "The main one is right in the middle of the song." She looked at the sopranos and smiled.

"Chaya," she said, "the second stanza of the song is going to be our main solo. Let's see what you can do with it."

We all looked over at Chaya. She looked nervous.

"Step forward, please," Miss Sperling instructed.

"Okay. Let me hear you."

Chaya clasped her hands together. She gazed off into the distance, as if she were standing alone in the middle of a field somewhere. And then she started singing.

What can I say? Her voice was like a skylark, swooping into the wide blue yonder.

Her voice was like a clear waterfall, spilling gracefully over a mountain cliff.

Her voice was like bells, chiming in the wind.

Her voice was... just right.

Miss Sperling seemed to think so, too. About one-third of the way through Chaya's solo audition, the instructor's head started nodding in a pleased way. At the halfway point, her eyes started shining. And when Chaya finished, Miss Sperling exclaimed, "Perfect! I don't think we need look any further, do we, girls?"

All around me, heads bobbed, and voices murmured, "Amazing!" or "Perfect!"

But something very different came out of my mouth. "It figures..."

I didn't think anyone heard me. But apparently, someone did.

And that someone was Miss Sperling herself.

"Ora?" she asked. "Do you have a problem?"

I hesitated. Then I looked down at the floor and muttered, "No."

She checked her watch again. "Girls, I'm going to let you out a few minutes early. Go straight to the parking lot to wait for your rides." As I picked up my backpack and started for the door with the others, she was suddenly at my side.

"Please stay here, Ora," she said quietly. "I want to talk to you."

I waited miserably until every last girl except for me was out of the room. When we were alone, Miss Sperling looked at me unhappily. "You seem to have a problem with my choosing Chaya to be the soloist, Ora."

I tried to control myself. But it was too much to take in one day! I had just found out that Penny, who I thought of as my best friend in this school, had taken Chaya along with her on a Chol HaMoed trip. Chaya was prettier than me, she had a better voice than me, and my best friend seemed to like her better than me.

And now, that same Chaya had been chosen to be the star of our show. It just wasn't fair!

"It's not fair!" I blurted. "You didn't even try out any other girls. It was just, 'Chaya, go ahead,' and then, 'Chaya, you got the part.' What about the rest of us?"

Miss Sperling was looking even more unhappy. "It's about being a team player, remember? Not about who gets to do what. It's about the good of the *whole*."

I gave her a blank stare.

"I think it would be a good idea for us to go down to Mrs. Mammon's office," Miss Sperling said. "She'll be able to explain it to you."

"No need for that," came a voice from the door. "I'm already here."

We both spun around. There, framed in the doorway, stood the principal herself.

As we gaped at her, Mrs. Mammon came into the room and strode over to join us.

Chapter 27

A Team Player

"**W**e have to make this fast," Miss Mammon said. "Your van will be ready to leave soon… But when I saw your girls pouring out of the choir room early, Miss Sperling, I decided to investigate. Is there a problem I can help with?"

"I think so," Miss Sperling said. She shot me a glance and then looked back at the principal. "Ora is upset that I gave Chaya the main solo in the song we're learning."

Both women turned to look at me. I tried not to squirm. They seemed to be waiting for an explanation, so I tried to give them one.

"Chaya is so… perfect," I muttered. "The way she looks. The way she sings. It doesn't seem fair that she should get *everything*!"

Mrs. Mammon and Mrs. Sperling exchanged a look. Then Mrs. Mammon said, "I think I'm hearing a little bit of jealousy here. Is that true?"

I couldn't think of a way to deny it. Anyway, what would be the point? I'd made it pretty obvious already. So I just nodded, staring down at my shoes.

"I have two things to say to you, Ora." The principal's voice was gentle, but there was a thread of steel behind them. "First, as Miss Sperling said, our performances are a *team effort*. We're part of something bigger than each of us alone. Bigger than our likes and dislikes." She stared deep into my eyes, willing me to take what she was saying into my heart and live with it. "We all want our performance to be as good as it can be — and for that to happen, everyone has to pull together. *Not* pull apart because they're unhappy with their personal share. Do you understand what I'm saying?"

I nodded again. I did understand. Sort of.

"Now, about the jealousy…"

I clenched up inside. I wished Miss Sperling wasn't there, listening to every word. I wished *I* wasn't there. Any place would be better than here. This was so mortifying!

Still, I was interested to hear what Mrs. Mammon had to say. She was a very smart lady. Could she help me with this problem that had been tearing me apart since… forever?

The principal told me, "I once heard a wise person say this: Jealousy is like a room. You can decide to walk in — or you can walk right past the door. *It's your choice*, Ora."

"But I *can't* walk past! It's too hard!" I felt like a baby, but all I could say was the truth.

"I know it's hard. We all have *middos* that are hard for

us to change. It may take you the rest of your life to conquer this one, Ora. But conquer it you must. Or you'll live a very sad sort of life, *chas v'shalom*."

I finally looked up, to find both Mrs. Mammon and Miss Sperling gazing at me with compassion in their eyes.

"I'll try," I whispered.

"Good," Mrs. Mammon said. "Remember, your emotions are not in charge of you. You can control *them*."

I nodded.

"Now," she said. "About the other thing." She turned stern again. "You disrupted choir practice because you weren't happy about someone else getting a solo. Your negative attitude could rub off on the others, and then where would we be?"

"I'm sorry," I mumbled.

"I hope you are," Mrs. Mammon said firmly. "When we talk about being team players, we mean it. We're going to keep an eye on you, Ora. Any more outbursts like the one you had today, and there could be a real problem."

"A p-problem?" My voice shook.

"Yes. This is a special kind of school, and it demands a special kind of behavior. You're going to have to show us that you have what it takes."

I once had a friend whose brother pulled a prank at school, and he was put on probation. He had to prove that he could behave better before they would let him stay in his school. I swallowed hard, and found the courage to ask Mrs. Mammon, "Am I on… probation?"

She didn't answer directly. All she did was repeat, "We're going to keep an eye on you. You're going to have to turn your attitude around, Ora. Okay?"

I nodded. I wanted to tell her that I would be a whole different person from now on, if only she would please, please, not kick me out of JAPA! But I didn't get a chance to say anything, because Mrs. Mammon said, "Now, hurry out to meet your van, Ora. And let's have a better day tomorrow."

The only response to that was "*Amein.*" So I said it.

Two minutes later I was waiting in line to board the van that would take me home.

In the busy parking lot, I saw Penny and Chaya waiting for their carpool. I saw Shayna spinning around like a dreidel to the tune of her "I'm so special song," which didn't sound nearly as charming to me as it had that morning. I saw girls in my choir giving me covert glances, which I tried to ignore.

When I remembered how happy I'd been, standing in a patch of sunlight in our kitchen that morning and looking forward to my first day back at school, I wanted to cry.

What a day this had been! I'd had two strikes already.

Strike one: finding out that Chaya had gone to the amusement park with Penny and her family… and then Penny lecturing me about being a nicer person.

Strike two: messing up so badly in choir that the principal had to give me a talking-to. A possible probation. *We're going to keep an eye on you, Ora.*

One more strike, and I'd be out. But what else could go wrong today?

Finally, it was my turn to climb onto the van and sit back for the ride home. It had been a long, long day, and I couldn't wait for it to be over.

But it wasn't over yet.

What else could go wrong? I asked myself.

The answer was: plenty. As I was about to find out.

I was quiet at supper, but no one seemed to notice.

Binny rushed in late, all flushed and sweaty from a basketball game at his friend Yitzi's house, and Mommy sent him off to wash up before he joined us at the table. Bassi entertained us with some more funny lines from my mother's old friend who was now Bassi's teacher.

Right before he left for Minchah and Maariv, Abba asked me quietly if I was okay. "You didn't say much at the table," he remarked.

"Just tired," I said.

"Better make it an early night then," he said with a smile. He put on his hat and jacket and left through the front door.

I was up in my room about an hour later, trying to concentrate on some homework, when the door flew open and Binny burst inside. His face was as red now as it had been after his game at supper. But this time, it was not red from playing. His cheeks were crimson with fury.

"It's all your fault!" he yelled, pointing an accusing finger at me.

I blinked. "What is?"

"I'm being grounded for a *whole week* — and it's all because of you!"

"What?" I was stunned. Reeling.

"You told Mommy and Abba that I tried to climb

Mr. Grossbaum's fence, even though you *said* you wouldn't!"

"Binny, I never —"

But Binny wasn't interested in hearing what I had to say. With blazing eyes, he shouted, "I *trusted* you! And you betrayed me. You are the worst sister in the world!"

With that, he left my room — slamming the door so hard that the whole house shook.

I stared at the door in a daze. I couldn't wrap my brain around what had just happened. For the third time that day, I was in the doghouse — and this time, it wasn't even my fault. After his fall from Mr. Grossbaum's fence, Binny had promised never to try to climb it again. I'd given him my word that I would keep the incident to myself.

And I'd kept my word. I hadn't breathed a word to our parents, or anyone else, about Binny climbing that fence. Not one syllable.

I had no idea how Mommy and Abba found out about it. But I did know one thing.

Three strikes — you're out.

Chapter 28
Triple Whammy

I put on my pajamas and curled up under the covers, shivering the way I did last winter when I had the flu. I could hear the rest of the house humming with activity, but as far as I was concerned it might as well have been the middle of the night.

I hugged my knees to my chest and tried not to cry.

Then I gave up trying, and let the tears leak out of my eyes. First one or two, and then a whole flood of them. So much had gone wrong that day that I didn't know what to think about first.

I sat there with my arms around my soggy knees and tried to think. It was important to figure this all out. To understand what had happened to me today, and why.

My mind traveled back to the last minute that I could remember being happy. When the world, and my life, had seemed full of light. It was the minute before Chaya started talking about something that had happened at the amusement park... when she'd been there with Penny.

Penny had tried to signal Chaya to stop talking. She'd known how bad I would feel about being left out. And I *had* felt bad. I felt awful.

But not as awful as I felt when Penny told me it was all *my* fault that she had invited Chaya and not me.

If only you wouldn't make it so hard...

You become someone else... someone mean.

Was I mean? I didn't mean to be. All I wanted was to be best friends with Penny and enjoy my time at JAPA. Was that too much to ask?

It looked like maybe it was.

The room was dark, but I pulled the covers over my head anyway. As if it hurt too much to see the world right then... or maybe because I didn't want the world to see *me*. I thought about how I reacted to what Penny said. I'd lashed out and blamed Penny for dumping me just because she found Chaya. But I knew that wasn't what really happened.

What had really happened was that Penny wanted *two* friends, but I wanted to be the only one. The special one.

I wanted to feel like — a *first* fiddle!

I heaved a sigh that seemed to travel all the way up from the soles of my feet. But that wasn't the end of my problems. There was plenty more to weigh me down. Like what had happened in my beloved choir. The choir that I was probably going to be kicked out of, right before I got kicked out of school.

The pain in my heart reminded me of the time I'd been six years old, and even though I knew I was not allowed to use a sharp knife I did anyway and accidentally slashed my finger with the knife. There was a really sharp sting, like a bee bite, followed by a long, throbbing ache. Right now, I was still in the stinging stage. Every time I thought about Miss Sperling and Mrs. Mammon, it felt like a knife stabbing me all over again.

Was it wrong to resent the way Chaya had everything that I wished *I* had?

Mrs. Mammon seemed to think so. She seemed to think that I had a choice about whether or not to be jealous of Chaya — or of anyone.

Jealousy is like a room…

Mrs. Mammon wanted me to walk past the door to that room instead of opening it up and going inside. *It's your choice, Ora.*

But it didn't *feel* like I had a choice. When I was jealous, it was as if the whole world narrowed down so that I could see only one tiny slice of it — and that slice was filled with the person I was jealous of. I couldn't see anything. I couldn't think of anything else. How was I supposed to change that?

I didn't have a clue.

And then, like a cherry on top of the day's whole disastrous cake, there was my brother's accusation. *I trusted you, Ora!*

Binny was furious with me. I didn't deserve his anger, but I didn't have the energy to try and fight it. Not now. Not today. This awful day of the triple whammy, weighing down on me like a whole herd of elephants.

The door opened. I heard it, but I couldn't see it because my head was still under the covers.

"Ora?" Bassi asked in a hushed voice. "Are you awake?"

"*Mmmff,*" I grunted.

"I can't believe you went to bed already. It's so early!"

"Go away," I mumbled.

"Are you okay?"

I pulled the blankets off my face and snarled, "No I'm *not* okay. I won't be okay until everyone just *leaves me alone*!"

I threw the covers over my head again and burrowed back down. Deep down, into the darkness and the misery. I heard Bassi leave the room, like I'd asked her to. That was good.

But I didn't *feel* good. "Good" was a trillion miles away just then.

In my nest of blankets, in the dark of my room, I felt more alone than I'd ever felt before in my life.

Chapter 29

All Up to Ora

When the door opened a second time, I resigned myself to another interrogation from my sister. Instead, I heard my mother's voice.

"Ora?"

With a sigh, I poked my head out of the covers again. Slowly, I wriggled into a sitting position. "What?"

Mommy came over to sit at the edge of my bed. "Do you mind if I turn on the lamp?"

"Whatever," I muttered.

Mommy reached out to switch on the lamp near my bed, then turned to gaze at me. "Bassi is worried about you," she said. "You don't usually go to bed this early."

I shrugged. "I was tired."

My mother's cool hand came up to rest on my forehead. "You don't have a fever."

I looked down at the twin lumps of my knees under the blankets. My lower lip began to quiver. *I will not cry.*

I will not cry. I will not —

The next thing I knew, those twin knee bumps were being treated to a storm. A storm of tears. Twin damp patches quickly formed where my knees stuck up under the covers.

Mommy's arms came around me. She made the soothing sounds that mothers make when you're hurting. Somehow, magically, they actually made some of the pain go away. But not all of it. Not even most of it.

"Talk to me, Ora," my mother said, when the storm had finally turned into a drizzle. "What's going on?"

I didn't want to talk about it — but I didn't want to keep it inside even more. So I started telling her about my problems. All except the part about Binny. I'd promised him not to tell our parents about his escapade with the fence if he promised never to climb it again. And I wanted to keep my word.

But I had plenty of other stuff to share. About Penny inviting Chaya to go to the park with her family on Chol HaMoed instead of me…

About Chaya getting the solo in choir…

About my reaction to that, and Miss Sperling's and Mrs. Mammon's reaction to *my* reaction.

"I'm such a loser," I sobbed against Mommy's shoulder. "I wish Chaya wasn't in our school. Then none of this would have happened."

My mother pulled back so she could see my swollen, tear-blotched face.

"This is not because of Chaya," she said firmly. "Chaya has nothing to do with it."

"What do you mean? Chaya's the one who's taking

Penny away from me! Chaya's the one who got the solo instead of me! Chaya —"

"If it wasn't Chaya, it would be someone else," Mommy said. "It's not any one person who's your enemy, sweetie. It's your own jealousy. Can't you see that?"

Oddly enough, now that she'd said it — I *could* see it.

I could see how sad it made me to always be jealous of the people in my life. First Bassi, then this girl or that in my old class… and now Chaya. There was always someone who made me green with envy. Would I ever be able to just be chilled?

"Mrs. M-mammon said it's like a r-room," I said with a hiccough. "She said I have a choice about whether or not to go in."

"She's right," Mommy said.

"But I can't *help* going in! It doesn't feel like I have a choice!"

My mother took a minute to think about that. "Maybe," she said slowly, "it's hard to resist going into the jealousy room when the door is standing wide open."

"Exactly!"

"So what you have to do," she told me, "is never, ever, open the door."

Slowly, I nodded my head. I had just realized something. Something huge.

This was up to me.

I couldn't sit back and wait for other people to solve this problem for me. Not my parents, not my teachers, not my principal or family or friends.

It was up to me, Ora M. Weiss, to tackle this humongous problem inside me. And, in Mrs. Mammon's words, to conquer it.

Mommy was looking at me as if she knew there were big things going through my head. She tilted her own head sideways and asked me an odd question.

"Do you trust Hashem?"

"What? Of course I do!"

"Do you believe that He loves you?"

I nodded my head.

"And that He gives everyone what they need to succeed in life?"

"Sure."

"And that He's the One Who showered you with all the blessings in *your* life?"

I nodded again, thinking about those blessings. You can forget them sometimes, when you're busy looking at what other people have.

"Hashem has given you so much, Ora. It's time to stop comparing yourself to other people and to focus on how much *you* have. Count your blessings. And after that..." She stopped.

"What, Mommy?" I prompted.

"After that," my mother said softly, "you have to learn how to share."

She went away a few minutes later, leaving me to turn off the lamp and stare into the darkness.

I thought about all the things I had to learn. Not to compare myself to other people. To remember to count my blessings.

To share?

I wasn't sure why Mommy had said that one, but I

added it to the list. So many things to do. So many ways I had to change.

I knew that I'd never be able to do it alone.

And that's why, just before I said *Shema* and fell asleep, I whispered, "Hashem, I really need You. Please help me get this right."

I don't remember falling asleep. But when I woke up, the sun was shining on my pillow, like a message of hope.

Chapter 30

Going It Alone

I wish I could say that I jumped out of bed and smilingly greeted the brand-new day. But I can't say it, because it wouldn't be true.

The truth? Getting out of bed that morning was one of the hardest things I've ever done. And getting on the van was even harder.

I didn't want to go to school. I couldn't bear the thought of having to face Penny. Or Chaya. Or Miss Sperling. Or Mrs. Mammon. Or the whole choir!

I'd messed up so badly the day before that I didn't see how I could live it down. All I wanted to do was keep on hiding under the covers until people forgot about my mess-ups and let me have a do-over.

And besides my mess-up in choir, there was the tiny fact that I'd basically lost my closest friend at school. I was friendly with other girls in my class, but it seemed that Penny was out of the picture. Her speech had left no doubt in my mind that she was just not interested anymore.

So, yes, it was hard to face the day.

But I did it anyway. I got out of bed, got dressed, and got ready for school. If I didn't do it today, I'd only have to face the ordeal tomorrow. Better, I figured, to just get it over with.

At breakfast, I returned Bassi's worried "Hi, Ora" with a small smile that was more like a grimace. I accepted Mommy's good-bye hug with a resigned sigh. Then it was off to the van, where I tried to make conversation with my classmates. They were nice girls. I didn't mind listening to them talk and I even inserted a sentence of my own now and then. But I couldn't really participate in the talk, because my mind was too full of other things.

Mostly, it was full of questions.

I was wondering how I was going to survive this day, with both the principal and my choir head busy "keeping an eye" on me because of my bad attitude, and Penny turning her back on me because I'd been mean to Chaya.

The sun didn't care about my problems. It shone brightly as our van rumbled through the early morning traffic, and winked off the mirrors of the cars we passed.

Each mile brought me closer to JAPA, and whatever I'd have to face when I got there.

The first thing I had to face was Shayna, doing her "We're so special" song and dance in the yard again.

By now, she had roped her classmates into joining her

— for the singing part, at least. Shayna whirled gracefully around in the middle of a circle of ninth graders, smiling as if she owned the world. Or at least the part of it that was in the schoolyard that morning.

Someone had added more lyrics to Shayna's song. It now included a description of how amazing the ninth graders were. How our school was special, but they were *extra*-special.

I tried to ignore them as I made my way from the van to the building. It wasn't easy, since they were taking up the whole middle of the yard. Aviva, Fraidy, and Layala, who had been on my van, followed me to the door. I guess they didn't feel so comfortable hanging around in the yard with all those *amazing* ninth graders.

Suddenly, I heard Shayna stop singing and start chanting, "Look at the seventh-grade babies. Look at the seventh-grade babies..."

Maybe she did that because we didn't give her the attention she wanted. I don't know. But her classmates joined right in, until the whole bunch of them were crooning about us poor, "seventh-grade babies." I heard someone behind me, Fraidy maybe, give a gasp. I could feel every ninth-grade eye boring a hole in my back. But I held my head high and led the way into the school building.

On the way in, I noticed the principal, Mrs. Mammon, coming out of her office to stand by the door. She was always on hand to greet us when the bell rang and the students started streaming in.

"Hello, girls," she said.

"Hi, Mrs. Mammon," my classmates chorused back.

"Hi," I mumbled, eyes down to avoid looking at her.

The memory of the principal's speech to me the day before echoed in my head, loud and clear.

I noticed that the chanting in the yard had stopped. Someone must have spotted Mrs. Mammon at the door. I wondered if the principal had heard what they were saying.

I didn't much like the way Shayna and her friends had treated us, but I refused to dwell on it too much. I had enough problems on my plate.

Anyway, Shayna and the other ninth graders could have saved themselves the trouble of trying to cut me down to size. I already felt small enough.

Chapter 31

Talks and Thrills

Mrs. Mammon had plenty to do over the course of the school day. She had to make sure the classes ran properly and on time. She had to speak to teachers, and parents, and the school board. And she had to take care of any problems that might crop up.

Like the one with Ora Weiss at choir the previous afternoon.

Or the one with Shayna Korman in the school yard this morning.

"Mrs. Mammon!" Yesterday, the school secretary had burst into her office, all pink in the face because she'd hurried the whole way. "I just heard one of the ninth graders singing a song that you would *not* approve of!"

"What kind of song?" Mrs. Mammon asked patiently.

Mrs. Reingold described the "We're so special" song, and the dance that Shayna liked to do in the schoolyard. "She and her friends are making a big deal about how special they are. They're being a bad influence on the younger girls, Mrs. Mammon."

Mrs. Mammon didn't like it. The song smacked of arrogance and showing off — two things that the principal wanted to keep her girls away from at all costs.

She had also heard rumors about how Shayna and her friends lorded it over their younger schoolmates. Another way of being arrogant...

She'd known, when she started JAPA, that a school for performing arts could impact the girls' *middos* in a negative way. That they might start thinking that they were better than other girls. Shayna Korman seemed to have fallen right into that trap.

So this morning, Mrs. Mammon had made sure to keep an eye on the yard before school started. Sure enough, there was Shayna, dancing away in the middle of a circle of her friends and singing her song. "We're so special...!"

She didn't want to say anything to Shayna yet. She hoped that this was just a stage. That Shayna and her friends would soon forget about their silly song and turn their attention elsewhere. But was that the responsible thing to do?

"This was exactly what I was afraid of when we started this school," she told the secretary now, worriedly. "I don't want our students to think that they're better than other girls just because they can sing or dance or play an instrument. I want them to be grateful to Hashem and humble about their talents. Not arrogant, *chas v'shalom!*"

"Most of them are just fine, I think," Mrs. Reingold said, trying to reassure the principal.

"Most of them," Mrs. Mammon agreed with a sigh. "But not all."

There and then, she decided to have a talk with Shayna. She would try to nip this thing right in the bud, before it spread to the other students and grew completely out of control.

"Shayna?" Mrs. Reingold had been standing at the foot of the steps, eyes peeled for a glimpse of Shayna as she returned to class after recess. "The principal wants to see you."

Even for a girl as confident as Shayna was, those words were ominous. She turned a little paler. Without a word to her friends or the secretary, she changed directions and headed for the office.

"Are we clear?" Mrs. Mammon asked Shayna, after they'd been talking — or mostly the principal had — for about ten minutes.

Shayna nodded sullenly. Even though she'd said she was clear about what the principal wanted, she felt the need to defend herself. "It was just a dance."

"It was just a dance *and* a song. A song about how special you and your classmates are."

Shayna looked down at her lap.

"And also how superior you are — to everyone else in this school," Mrs. Mammon went on.

Still Shayna said nothing.

"You know something? It's true," the principal said, surprising her. "You girls *are* special."

Shayna's eyes grew round. "We are?"

"Yes." The principal leaned forward. *"As special as everyone else around here."*

Shayna let out her breath and looked away.

"There are some beautiful dances and songs in the world," Mrs. Mammon said quietly. "You are very talented, Shayna. I'm sure you can come up with a better one."

She waited, but Shayna had nothing to say.

"Are we clear?" Mrs. Mammon repeated. "This will not happen again, right?"

"Right. I guess." Shayna's voice was almost inaudible.

Mrs. Mammon had just sent Shayna back to class with a note to explain her lateness when the phone rang. A moment later, the principal heard her secretary's voice coming through the inter-office intercom.

"There's a Mrs. Benstein on the phone for you," she said. "From London."

London?

"Hello?" Mrs. Mammon said into the phone.

She listened to what her caller had to say in a lovely English accent. As she listened, her eyes grew wider and wider.

"Thank you so much, Mrs. Benstein," she said at the end of the call. "We are so pleased that you called. I'm going to transfer you to my secretary, so she can make all the arrangements with you."

After she hung up, Mrs. Mammon stared into space for about five seconds. Then, slowly, a big smile spread across her face.

Wait until she told the others about this! They would be as thrilled as she was.

She quickly dashed off a message for the women in charge of the school's performing arts program. Miss Sperling, head of choir... Miss Judowitz, head of the orchestra… and Mrs. Danciger, who liked to laughingly say, "With a name like that, what else can I do but teach people how to dance?"

Their answers came quickly. As expected, all three of them were just as excited as the principal was. They were already working hard — but now they were determined to make the school's first performance the very best that it could be!

They tried to keep the news to themselves, but somehow it leaked out of the school office. It flew on wings, down the halls and into the classrooms. It fluttered among the girls in the school yard at recess. Pretty soon, it was the only thing anyone could talk about.

A woman who headed a famous *tzedakah* organization in London was going to be in New York on Chanukah — and she was interested in attending their first performance!

"We are *really* going to be famous," Shayna Korman said with satisfaction. She seemed to have forgotten all about her talk with the principal that morning.

And her oh-so-special classmates agreed with her — one hundred percent.

Chapter 32

Missing Ora

Penny made her way down to the basement, where she had fallen into the habit of spending the ten-minute break before music prep. It was a quiet spot in the bustling school, and she relished the chance to head down there for a few minutes at the end of the busy day.

This time, though, there was a difference. When the school year had started, she'd come down here with Ora. Now she was alone.

Ora had pretty much been avoiding her all day. In a way, Penny wasn't sorry about that. She wasn't sure what to do about the problem with Ora and Chaya, and this gave her some extra time to try to figure it out.

She'd spent most of her free time with Chaya today… but then Chaya had done a disappearing act, too.

"Want to go to the basement?" Penny had asked her, as they packed up their backpacks after the last bell.

"No — sorry — there's something I need to do," Chaya had answered quickly. Then, just as quickly, she'd swung her backpack over her shoulder and practically run out of the classroom.

Penny had stared after her. What was going on?

Shaking her head, she continued down to the basement on her own. With the distant sound of dozens of girls talking in the lobby above, this was like an oasis of peace and quiet. She set down her backpack and was about to investigate the janitor's room to see if Gali was there — when the door opened and Gali herself cartwheeled out.

"Whoa!" Penny said, laughing and ducking out of the way. "When did you learn how to do that?"

"When I was little. I used to cartwheel all over the place before I came to this school," Gali said breathlessly.

"So why'd you stop?"

Gali sank down next to Penny on the floor, her long ponytail hanging down over her shoulder. "Things are different now. These days I have to be very careful. If I hurt myself turning cartwheels, *chas v'shalom*, I won't be able to dance. And then where would I be?"

Penny thought about this. Playing the flute at JAPA was no different than playing it at home. She never worried about not being able to play. Poor Gali! Penny wished that the other girl wouldn't worry so much.

"You'll be fine," she said comfortably. "Millions of people dance and do cartwheels every day and are just fine!"

"Yeah," Gali said gloomily. "But there's always the one-in-a-million chance that something could go wrong."

What Penny might have answered will never be known.

At that moment, they were interrupted by the sound of footsteps. They were coming down to the basement.

An instant later, two figures appeared on the landing. Seeing who they were, Penny's heart sank.

"Hi!" she called up to the ninth graders, trying to sound chipper.

Shayna put her hands on her hips and let out a huff. "It's those seventh graders again," she told her friend Brachi in a long-suffering voice. She spoke as if Penny and Gali couldn't hear her. "They seem to think they *own* the basement."

"There's plenty of room for more," Penny called. "Feel free to join."

"*Join* you guys?" Shayna sniffed. "As if." She turned to go, her faithful shadow following right behind her. The principal's message about not feeling superior to other people seemed to have gone right over her head.

Penny rolled her eyes at Gali, as if to say, *What can you do if people refuse to be friendly*? To comfort herself, she pulled a bag of jellybeans out of her backpack and held it out to Gali. "Want some?"

Gali looked at the candy as if it were a bag of poison. "That is *so* bad for you," she said earnestly.

"Well, I don't eat them all day. Just a couple of jellybeans now and then. Go ahead, have a treat!"

"Why don't you have one of *my* treats? It's much healthier." And Gali pulled a granola bar out of her backpack. It seemed to be chock-full of healthy ingredients. It also looked utterly unappetizing.

"Uh, maybe some other time," Penny said, shaking her head with a smile. She poured a handful of jellybeans into her palm and began searching for a red one.

Even with Gali right next to her munching on a granola bar, Penny felt a little lonely. She wondered where Chaya was. She wished Chaya were here instead.

Ever since they'd started carpooling together, she and Chaya had been spending a lot of time together. Chaya was one of the nicest girls she'd ever met. Never a mean word to say about anyone. She was a beautiful person, inside and out. Penny admired her and she definitely enjoyed her company.

But there was another, deeper reason for Penny's loneliness. And it was time to face it.

She missed Ora.

She had liked Ora from the first second they met by the bus on the last day of camp. When they found themselves in the same school *and* living in the same neighborhood, although some distance apart, Penny had been sure they would be the closest of friends. And, at first, it seemed to be happening.

Then came that awful Shabbos. The afternoon when both Ora and Chaya had visited Penny at home. Chaya had been fine — but Ora? She'd acted as if Chaya wasn't even there. Or as if she *wished* she wasn't there.

I tried to talk to her, Penny thought sadly. *I asked her how she could be so mean. But it was as if Ora didn't even hear me...*

As long as Ora continued to be so stubborn about keeping Chaya out in the cold, Penny didn't see how they could stay friends. It was as simple as that.

As simple — and as complicated — as that.

She and Gali chatted a bit, but mostly they were quiet,

busy with their snacks and their thoughts. When the secretary's voice over the intercom announced that it was time for music prep, Penny was glad to go.

She would play her flute in the orchestra and let the music carry her away from her troubled thoughts for a while.

But she knew that they would still be waiting for her when she came back down to earth.

Chapter 33

Useless Efforts

C haya paused in front of the door she wanted. She looked over her shoulder to make sure no one was around to see her. The corridor was empty. Everyone was either milling around in the lobby during these precious ten minutes of freedom, or hanging out on the front lawn. Penny was probably down in the basement. She'd wanted Chaya to come with her.

Not today, Chaya thought. She had something more important to do than chill with Penny right now. She had a mission to carry out — and there wasn't a minute to waste!

She lifted a nervous fist and rapped on the door.

"Yes? Come in!"

Slowly, Chaya pushed open the door. Miss Sperling glanced up from some sheets of music. She looked surprised.

"Chaya? You're here early. Rehearsal doesn't start for

ten more minutes." She glanced at the clock on the wall. "Nine minutes now."

"I know," Chaya said. "I came early because — because I wanted to ask you something."

"Oh?" Miss Sperling put down the music and gave the girl her full attention. "I'm listening."

"It's about the solo."

"The solo?"

"You know — the solo in the song we just learned. The one you decided to give to me."

"Oh, that solo," Miss Sperling said. "What about it? Do you need some help with the harmony?"

"No, I'm fine with the harmony."

Chaya seemed to be having a hard time getting to the point. Miss Sperling decided to help her along. "So... if you know the harmony, what's the problem?"

Chaya looked up at her. "Ora," she said, almost whispering.

"Ora?"

"Remember how upset she was when you gave me the solo?"

Miss Sperling pressed her lips together. "Ora's a great kid, but she needs to work on not being so jealous. That solo is yours, fair and square."

"But I don't want it!" Chaya burst out.

Miss Sperling was taken aback. "Why ever not?"

Chaya's next words came in a whisper. "I'd rather not have the solo than have Ora be so upset."

"Upset at *you*?" Miss Sperling asked shrewdly.

Chaya shrugged. "All I know is — she's not happy. I'll gladly give up the solo if it'll make her happy."

"But it won't make *me* happy," Miss Sperling said, her voice gentle but firm. "It won't make me happy because I want what's best for the choir. *And* for Ora."

"What do you mean?" Chaya asked, startled.

"You want to make Ora happy by giving up what you have. I think it would be much better to let Ora learn how to be happy with her *own* portion. She may get a solo down the road, but I gave this one to you."

"But —"

"It was very nice of you to offer to give up the solo," Miss Sperling said. "But the offer is refused."

"But —"

"The solo is yours, Chaya. Let's give Ora a little time. I'm sure she'll be okay with it."

Chaya sighed. She was not nearly as sure as Miss Sperling seemed to be.

"So, how many days are you grounded?" Yitzi asked Binny as they left the school building at the end of the day.

"I still have three more days to go. Till Wednesday," Binny answered gloomily.

It had been a Wednesday night when his parents told him that they knew he'd tried to climb Mr. Grossbaum's fence, and that he was to be grounded as a consequence. That meant no playing in Yitzi's yard for *a whole week*.

His mother and father didn't tell him *how* they knew about his escapade with the fence. But they didn't have to. He already knew.

No one but his sister Ora had known about it. She was the one who saw him trying to deal with the scrape he'd received when he fell off the fence. She had cleaned the scrape and bandaged it for him. He'd been grateful to her for that.

He'd been even more grateful when she agreed not to tell their parents if he promised never to do it again. And he had kept his promise... but *she* had broken hers!

Ora must have decided to tell Mommy and Abba about it after all. Probably thought she was being a responsible big sister or something. He was furious with her for that. A promise is a promise!

But Binny was not the kind of kid who gives up so easily. He had a plan.

Walking into the house after school, he gave his mother a big smile, "Hi, Ma!"

"Hi, Binny. How was school today?"

"It was fine. When's supper?"

"In a few minutes. We're having meatballs and spaghetti."

"*Yes*! My favorite!"

His mother smiled.

"Want me to set the table?" Binny asked.

His mother was surprised, and Binny didn't blame her. It was not every day that he volunteered to do chores around the house. In fact — to be perfectly honest — it was not *any* day that he volunteered to do chores around the house.

"Let me get this straight. You're offering to set the table? Without being asked?" she said incredulously.

"Sure." Binny nodded his head virtuously. He was

hoping that, if his behavior was good enough, his parents would change their minds and *un*-ground him.

"Well, thank you, Binny. I appreciate the help," Mommy said.

But a "thank you" was *all* he got. Even though he set the table for supper *and* cleared it afterward, neither his mother nor his father said a word about taking away his punishment.

Binny scowled. It was no use. He had to face the fact that he was stuck in the house all by himself this week while his friends were living it up in Yitzi's back yard. Yitzi's father had rigged up a strong light so they could play even now, when the days got dark early. As they had played after school yesterday. And today.

They were practicing on Yitzi's hoop every day, learning how to throw baskets better and better, while he fell way behind. Pretty soon, Yitzi wouldn't even let him play with them, because they'd all be so much better than he was.

He clenched his fists. It wasn't fair! He was going to be left out of everything.

And it was *all Ora's fault.*

Chapter 34

Where's the Happiness?

The principal and Miss Sperling were going to keep an eye on me, and Penny was disappointed in me. I woke up the next morning wondering: How in the world was I going to get through the day?

In the end, I got through it mostly by keeping to myself.

I avoided Penny, which wasn't too hard as she seemed to be doing the same to me.

And I stayed away from places where the principal was likely to be.

Thank goodness, there was no choir practice that afternoon. It would have been hard to face Mrs. Sperling after what had happened the last time we met. Instead, we had a voice training session with Mrs. Wexler.

"Your vocal cords, girls," she told us, "are two bands of muscle in your larynx. That's your voice box."

I pictured my voice sitting inside a box, all decorated like one of those music boxes that you wind up to make a pretty tune float out.

"Air comes up from your lungs and passes through the cords, making them vibrate," Mrs. Wexler continued. "That's what makes the sound of your voice."

I raised my hand. "Why are some voices higher or lower than others?" I asked curiously.

"That depends on a few things. Whether you're a boy or a girl, for one. And the thickness of the vocal cords," Mrs. Wexler said.

After that, she taught us how to breathe. You'd think a twelve-year-old girl would already be an expert on breathing. Even a baby can do that without any help. But apparently there's more to breathing than I realized.

When it comes to singing, there is a right way and a wrong way to do everything — even breathe!

"You have to learn how to control your breathing," Mrs. Wexler declared.

"Why?" Devori asked.

"Breathing the right way will help you hold a note longer. And it will keep you from running out of air just when you need it. You don't want to be gasping for air in the middle of a song, do you?"

Devori's eyes grew wide. "Of course not!"

I pictured a choir full of girls looking like a bunch of fish out of the water, and gasping for air as we tried to sing.

"Of course not," Mrs. Wexler agreed. "Now," she said, "let me ask you a question. What's better — a weak voice or a strong one?"

Some of the girls looked like they wanted to say, "*Duh...*" Mrs. Wexler smiled. "Okay, let's go with strong. So how do you make your voice stronger?"

"Sing louder?" someone guessed.

"No. People make the mistake of thinking that they have to strain their throats if they want their voices to be more powerful," she said. "That's wrong. You're not supposed to strain. What you do is *support* your voice."

"Support them how?" I asked.

"By using other muscles in your body to prop up your voice." She gave us some examples. I thought about how Mrs. Sperling had called my voice "powerful." Had my muscles been supporting my voice without my even knowing it?

Then Mrs. Wexler had us sing the notes in a scale, over and over. When it was Chaya's turn, we all listened with pleasure — even me. She could make a simple scale sound like pure gold. We could have listened to her forever.

Mrs. Wexler taught us how to "rest" our voices on our diaphragm, and how to breathe so that our stomachs moved instead of our shoulders. It was all very fascinating, and for the space of the lesson I actually forgot about my problems. Even with Chaya right there in the room with me, sounding like a nightingale every time she opened her mouth to sing.

Then it was time for afternoon pick-up. As I trudged out of the school building behind a bunch of other girls, I felt all my problems flooding back again.

I saw Penny and Chaya waiting for their carpool. They seemed to be talking up a storm. I wondered if Penny even remembered that I existed anymore...

I felt more sad than mad. I figured I didn't really deserve Penny's friendship anyway. The words she'd said to me the day before were etched into my brain, as if someone had written them in indelible ink:

You become someone else... someone mean.

Chaya was a much nicer person than I was. Could I really blame Penny for preferring her company instead of mine?

No. I couldn't.

But that didn't mean I had to like it.

I brooded about my lack of friends on the drive home from school. The drive seemed extra-long tonight. There was more traffic than usual and everything seemed to be moving in slow-motion. It was good to finally get off the van and walk into my house.

But even that relief didn't last long. Every time I turned around, it seemed, there was my brother, giving me the cold shoulder.

"What's up with Binny?" Bassi asked me in our room later. "He's been acting weird tonight. Like he's mad or something."

"There's no 'something,' about it," I told her. "He *is* mad. At me."

"Why?" Bassi asked.

I shrugged. I'd promised not to tell anyone about what had happened when Binny tried to climb Mr. Grossbaum's fence, and I did not intend to break my promise. Even if Binny had accused me falsely and kept shooting daggers at me with his eyes all through supper.

I didn't want to think about Binny. Or about Chaya

and Penny. Or about choir. I just wanted to escape, some-where safe and peaceful where nothing could bother me. I decided to do it by re-reading an old favorite book and then — for the second time in two days — going to bed early.

But it was a long time before I fell asleep. I lay staring up in the dark as the thoughts I'd pushed away all eve-ning came rushing back. Thoughts about all the things that had gone wrong with my life. I could hardly believe how happy I'd been just a few days ago.

Where had all that happiness gone?

Chapter 35

A New Resolution

The next day was Friday, a short day with no music prep. Then came Shabbos. Naturally, I spent the whole afternoon imagining Penny and Chaya having fun together at one of their houses. I wished that I had thought to invite one or two of my other classmates over. I was so lonely that I almost wished that Lana and Shoshie would come by again! Anything would have been better than hanging around all by myself.

When Bassi came home late in the day from visiting her friends, she took pity on me and agreed to play a couple of board games. *Count your blessings*, Mommy always told me. I figured that Bassi was one of my blessings. She was almost always nice to me — even when all she got in return was a load of nasty jealousy.

I was grateful to her for spending time with me on that endless Shabbos afternoon, though I knew I didn't deserve her niceness. Afterward, though, I was right back where I'd been before: friendless. Alone.

When you get right down to it, there's nothing like a friend. Especially when you don't have one.

That night, I was about to get into bed when I remembered that I'd left my book downstairs. Coming quietly down the steps in my bare feet, I suddenly heard Mommy and Bassi in the living room. They were talking quietly, and normally I wouldn't have tried to overhear what they were saying.

But I did listen now… because I heard them say my name. They were talking about me.

"Ora's been so down in the dumps these past few days," Bassi said in a hushed voice. "Do you have any idea why? Did something happen?"

"I don't know the answer to that, Bassi. But I've also noticed that Ora's been in a bad mood lately."

"I don't know what to do with her." Bassi sighed. "Nothing I do cheers her up…"

"All you can do," Mommy said, "is keep on being a nice big sister to her."

"I try to be. But it's like she's so weighed down with her own feelings that she can hardly even *hear* me."

There was a short silence. Then my mother said, "People can get very caught up in their emotions, Bassi. It can make them a little… self-centered."

"So what do I do?"

I could hear the smile in Mommy's voice as she said, "Just wait it out. The good thing about a bad mood is that sooner or later, it's bound to turn around and become a good one!"

I stayed where I was, frozen, for a few seconds, as motionless as the staircase I was standing on. Suddenly, I realized that Bassi could walk out at any second and see me standing there! I forgot about the book I'd meant to fetch. Spinning around, I turned around and went quietly back to my room.

This isn't just a bad mood, I wanted to tell them. *This is my whole* life *falling apart!*

But I couldn't tell them that, because they didn't know I'd heard them talking.

All I could do was crawl into bed and cry in the dark until I fell asleep.

Sunday was another long, quiet day. It rained on and off all afternoon, which made it the right kind of day for staying cozily at home. The problem was, I had no one to be cozy with, and nothing cozy that I wanted to do.

I was on the couch, gazing out the window at the rain and doing what I was best at these days — moping — when my father came in and sat down beside me. "Why the long face, Ora?"

I didn't want to tell him.

I *did* want to tell him.

I didn't know what to do.

He just sat there, waiting. In the end, I mumbled, "I messed some things up."

Abba didn't answer right away. I liked that. It meant that he was thinking over what I'd just said.

"Everyone messes up sometimes," he said.

"*You* don't."

My father smiled. "Even me."

I found that hard to believe. Both of my parents seemed like — like finished products. All perfect and shiny, like something delivered straight from the factory in top-notch working condition. Me? I was like a half-sawed piece of lumber that *might*, if I was lucky, turn into something halfway decent one day.

Abba was saying something. I turned off my thoughts and started paying attention.

What he was saying was this: "Want to hear what I do when that happens?"

"When you mess up?" I asked.

He nodded.

"Sure." Like I said, I couldn't imagine Abba messing up. But I was curious to hear his answer.

"First, I ask Hashem to help me get it right next time. To help me fix the parts of me that led to the mess-up."

I nodded again, slowly. That made sense. Hashem knows how we feel inside. He knows about our bad *middos,* and about our good intentions. Who else but Hashem can help us get it right?

"And then," Abba continued, "I sit down and try to figure out which part of the mess-up was out of my control — and which part I actually helped make happen. And I think about what *I* can do to fix that part."

"I never know how to fix what I mess up," I said with a sigh.

He twinkled at me in a way that made me feel a little more hopeful.

"Not yet," he said.

I had the rest of the day to mull over what my father

had said. It hung out in the back of my mind until I finally turned out the light that night. Like a puzzle you haven't solved yet. Or a story whose ending you're dying to know.

Just before I went to sleep, I once again said a little *tefillah* to Hashem. I asked for His help in getting things right, because I sure didn't have a very good track record for getting them right on my own.

The thought made me sadder than ever — until I remembered what Abba had said. It gave me a tiny spark of hope.

Not yet...

And then it was Monday again. Back to school — with just seven weeks to go before our performance.

Our choir was going to work hard these next few weeks. We would try to perfect the harmony on the first song we'd learned, and then learn several new ones. Miss Sperling would expect us to be at our best. She always demanded that we be on time, that we pay attention, and that we learn our parts carefully and well.

Most of all, she insisted that we be team players. The most important thing Miss Sperling wanted us to bring to every practice was a good attitude.

I boarded the van to JAPA on that cloudy, windswept Monday morning filled with determination. I'd had plenty of time to think over the weekend, and I knew what I had to do.

I took a seat on the van. My classmates would board

a little later, but for now I was alone except for two girls in grades higher than me. Then and there, I made a resolution.

A singer needs to exercise her vocal cords to keep them strong. *I* would have to exercise, too — and not just my vocal cords. I had to work on strengthening a different but super-important muscle.

I might be a lonely girl in the market for a friend.

I might be on probation at my wonderful school.

I might have a brother who was furious with me for something I didn't do.

I might be the moodiest girl in the world.

But there was one thing that I was starting to learn from all of this. I was learning that there were a lot of things I couldn't control. But my attitude?

That was up to me.

Chapter 36

A Strange Encounter

School — even one that teaches performing arts — is still school. With Succos behind us, that meant plenty of homework. And plenty of tests.

"The teachers are really piling it on," Fraidy moaned on the van going home. "I don't know what to do first!"

"I'm dreading the Chumash test," Esti said, twitching her hair nervously from one shoulder to the other.

"*I'm* dreading math," Layala said with a shudder.

Secretly, I didn't mind the upcoming tests so much. In fact, being short of friends at the moment, I was actually kind of happy about it. Studying would give me something to do besides thinking about all the reasons I had to be sad.

Also, I had another hope. Even though I'd messed up in choir, maybe I could show Mrs. Mammon that I was at least a decent student.

"What about you?" Layala asked me. "What are *you* dreading?"

"All that homework," I said promptly. "Night after night after night of it."

My classmates nodded their heads in agreement. A test comes and a test goes — but homework is never done!

Now that the days were growing shorter, the drive back from school was less interesting. All I could see was a stream of headlights in front of us and the twinkling lights of buildings at the sides of the road. It was strange to think that each of those lights belonged to a whole family that I didn't know. It made me realize just how big the world is.

My own part in the world always seems so important to me, but I guess the part that belongs to other people seems just as important to *them*. It made me feel kind of humble, somehow. As if my stuff is not nearly as important as I think it is…

The long day, the darkness outside our windows, and the rumble of the wheels under our feet made us drowsy. Sooner or later, after we talked awhile, some of us usually ended up nodding off. Including yours truly.

I woke up when someone nudged me in the ribs and said, "Hey, Ora — it's your stop."

I said a sleepy good-bye and stumbled off the van. Except for the streetlights and the glow of light through some unshaded windows, the street was dark. The cool, crisp air was like a slap in the face and woke me up fast.

I was in a hurry. Mrs. Heimowitz, down the block, had asked me to babysit her kids for an hour because she had a late meeting at work. I ran into my house, called out "Hi!" to Mommy, dumped my backpack, called out "Bye!" to Mommy, and ran out again.

A minute later, I was knocking on the Heimowitzes' door.

"*Ora's here!*"

The three Heimowitz kids, aged two, four, and six, were all over me the second I walked in, begging me to play with them, read to them, listen to them. Four-year-old Tali started telling me an endless story about something or other, but before she'd said two sentences she was in a great big muddle, with all the details mixed up in her head and contradicting each other. Then little Nomi toddled over, carrying a pile of picture books almost as tall as she was. Mrs. Heimowitz waited until I was sitting on the couch like an island in a sea of kids and books, and then gave a quick wave and slipped out the door.

The next hour went by fast. After I read a few stories out loud, I asked Rina, the six-year-old, how she liked school. She said that she loved her *morah*. Then she asked me if loved *my morah*. I said that my teachers were fine, and told her a little about my unusual school. Rina was fascinated.

"I wish *I* had a school where you get to sing all day!" she pouted.

I laughed. "It's not exactly like that. Most of the time, it's just like any other school. We learn stuff all day and then practice our singing at the end of the day."

Rina was interested in hearing more. Her sisters, not so much. They wanted to play.

So we played hide-and-seek and other assorted kid games until their mother came back. She thanked me and paid me for my time, and then it was my turn to slip out the door when the kids' backs were turned.

The Heimowitzes lived only four doors down from us, so my parents were okay with my walking home alone so early in the evening. I strolled down the street, breathing in the chilly air and thinking about what I might do with the money I'd just earned. It was darker than usual because there was no moon, but I wasn't afraid.

That is, I wasn't afraid until — out of the darkness — someone called, "Excuse me? Miss?"

It was a man's voice. One that I didn't know. Goosebumps popped out on my arms and my heart went into overdrive. I was about to start running for home when the owner of the voice stepped into the light of the nearest streetlamp, and I saw who it was.

"Mr. Grossbaum!" I put a hand to my heart.

"Did I startle you? I'm sorry." He was wearing a light overcoat over his suit. His hair, what I could see of it, shone silver in the light of the streetlamp. "I just realized that I left my watch at home, so I wanted to ask if you know what time it is. My car is in the shop and I want to see if I have time to walk to shul in time for the next *minyan*."

I lifted my arm so the light so see what my watch said. When I told him, he nodded in a pleased way. "I've got plenty of time, then." He paused, considering me. "You're the Weiss girl, aren't you?"

I nodded.

"Binyamin's brother?"

I nodded again, more cautiously this time.

"The one who tried to climb my fence and ended up falling down?"

I stared at my neighbor. "How — how do you know about that? Binny said you weren't even home when it happened!"

"That's right, I went away for Succos. It was my neighbor who saw your brother, and she told me about it afterward. Is he all right?"

"Binny's fine. But he got in big trouble for trying to climb your fence."

Something in my voice must have sounded like an accusation, because Mr. Grossbaum peered at me in the dimness and said, "Tell me something, Miss Weiss. Do you think your brother did the right thing? Climbing my fence when I specifically asked your father to tell him not to?"

I hesitated. Part of me wanted to find a way to end the conversation and go home. This was none of my business, right? But another part wanted to stick up for Binny. He might be angry at me for no reason, but he was still my brother.

"Why does there even have to be a fence there in the first place?" I blurted.

His eyes narrowed. "Eh?"

"Um… I just mean that the fence makes life hard for my brother."

"How's that?"

"Binny's friend lives around the corner, and Binny really likes to play at his house along with some other friends. He always tries to get there fast because otherwise he won't get to play ball with them. All the neighbors let him take a shortcut through their back yards. All except you…"

"I see." Mr. Grossbaum's silvery head moved up and down. He looked at me. I looked down at the sidewalk. Then he said, "Thank you, Miss Weiss. You've given me something to think about."

I looked up. "I have?"

"Yes, indeed. I need to run to shul now, but I won't forget this talk. No, I won't forget…"

It was too dark to read the expression on his face. I didn't know if he meant what he'd said in a good way or a bad one. Had I just got Binny in even *more* trouble?

It had been such an odd encounter, running into this neighbor whom I hardly ever saw out here on the dark street. Our conversation had been strange, too. I turned it over in my mind as I walked home. By the time I got there, the whole thing had started to feel dreamlike. Like something that I could push into the back of my mind and forget about.

Which, before very long, was exactly what I did.

Chapter 37

Excitement in the Air

L ike a runaway snowball, the days began zooming past. We had classes, we had tests, and we had *tons* of homework. You'd think that a school for the performing arts would put practice first, and maybe cut down a little on the schoolwork.

Not JAPA.

"We want to prove that a school can be both!" Mrs. Mammon announced at one of our school assemblies. "We will *not* be known as a school with top-notch arts performances but a lackluster academic one.

"And that is why" — she leaned over her podium, her gaze sweeping over every single girl in that auditorium — "we are going to be extra strict about your grades. Anyone who finds herself failing a class will have to work very hard to improve. Because there is no place in our school for a student who does not take her schoolwork seriously."

Some of the girls around me looked nervous when they

heard this. It made me a little nervous, too. But not very much. When I bother to apply myself (as the teachers like to put it) I do okay. Maybe even better than just okay. There was no danger of my slacking off *now*, when I was on probation. I was determined to prove myself.

Much more exciting than schoolwork was choir practice. We learned two more songs and some fantastic harmonies. One afternoon, a woman with a measuring tape came to measure us for costumes. Real ones, not the simple colored sashes that our fifth-grade teacher tied around our waists to dress up the dark skirts and white blouses we wore for our amateur choir back then. This was the real thing. This was *professional*.

Walking through the halls, there was a kind of *buzz* in the air. I heard snatches of talk from girls who were in the dance group or the orchestra. Our choir was not the only thing being spruced up for the Chanukah performance. *Everyone* was going to wear custom-made costumes. The musicians were even getting special stands to hold their music scores. Everything was going to be as professional as it could be!

I wished I could run over to Penny to discuss it all. But she was sticking close to Chaya these days, and I was mostly sticking to myself. Now and then, I hung around with some of the other girls in my class. They were nice girls, but they had already paired up and formed their own groups. I didn't really feel that I fit into any of them. Besides, I missed Penny.

Mostly I kept sneaking peeks at her and Chaya at the other end of the lunchroom and wondering what they were talking about.

I kept telling myself not to look, but it was hard. I didn't know which would hurt more: seeing Penny looking perfectly happy without me, or not getting to see her at all...

I also spent a lot of time trying to prove to Miss Sperling that I was a team player.

In choir, I paid attention to everything she told us and basically sang my heart out. In our voice-training classes, I practiced scales until they were coming out of my ears. I listened to the other choir members sing and tried to learn from their techniques. I even got so used to hearing Chaya sing that I stopped being so jealous of it. If I let myself forget that she had stolen Penny from me, I could almost enjoy it. Almost.

It was still hard not to be envious. But Chaya's voice, I figured, was the thing that would really put our choir over the top. And an over-the-top choir was what we *all* wanted, right?

Like I said — a team player.

I tried to pick up clues from Miss Sperling about whether or not I was succeeding. I couldn't tell. She didn't act angry at me, but she also didn't act especially approving. It was as if she'd told herself "wait and see." As if she wouldn't take a stand, one way or the other, until she was sure.

I wished she would go ahead and make up her mind already. Here's something you might not know: being on probation is really hard on the nerves. If I even let myself *think* about it during choir practice, my voice dried up and I couldn't sing a note.

So I forced myself not to think about it. I was getting

better and better at this not-thinking thing. If it went on much longer, I'd probably be able to convince myself that my life was just hunky-dory. All sunny blue skies, with not a cloud in sight...

I made a wry face and sighed. Who was I kidding?

Math was our last class of the day. One afternoon, Mrs. Richter, our teacher, handed back our first test of the year. I was happy to see a big, red "98 — well done!" scrawled across the top of my test paper. But some of my classmates did not look so happy. Chaya took one look at her paper and turned white.

I remembered her saying how much she hated math, on the one Shabbos afternoon we'd spent together in Penny's house. I wondered what kind of mark was scrawled across the top of *her* test. From the look on her face, I figured it wasn't that great.

"Some of you did not do well on this test," Mrs. Richter said bluntly. She was the kind of person who said most things bluntly. "I suggest that you review the material carefully. Next week, I will be giving another test. It will include the material from this one — plus everything we've learned since then." She looked around the classroom and added grimly, "I wish you luck."

Echoes of Mrs. Mammon's speech seemed to fill the room. *Anyone who finds herself failing a class will have to work very hard to improve. Because there is no place in our school for a student who does not take her schoolwork seriously...*

A sense of doom filled the air.

"It's not fair," someone muttered. "They should cut us some slack! We're so busy rehearsing for the performance."

"This is a school for the performing arts," Mrs. Richter snapped. "You will *always* be rehearsing for one performance or another. That is no excuse for sloppy work!"

With those words ringing in our ears, we heard the bell ring for the end of the class.

"Music prep in ten minutes," the secretary's voice droned over the intercom, the way it did every day. It was time to gather our things, troop out of the room, and scatter to the four winds.

Chaya, I noticed, was the first one out the door.

Chapter 38

A Mystery

Chaya walked down the hall as fast as she could. All the other girls in her class had rushed toward the steps that would take them down to the lobby and then the music prep rooms. That was why Chaya decided to go in the opposite direction instead.

She walked until she reached the last classroom at the end of the hall. There she stopped and listened for a moment. All was quiet. Pushing open the door a crack, she cautiously peeked in. There was no one there. On the blackboard were scribbled a few dates, which made her think there had been a history class here sometime today. But the room was empty now. She slipped inside.

She barely made it to the nearest desk before she burst into tears.

Blinded by the tears, she dropped her backpack to the floor and buried her face in her arms. The rest of the world seemed to move far away. All she could hear were her shuddering sobs, and all she could see was the darkness behind her closed eyelids. The desk was hard beneath her arms and her sleeves were slowly becoming damper by the minute.

For a long time, she was too busy crying to think about anything at all. But, soon enough, the thoughts came. And they were not happy ones.

Why, oh why, had she ever thought she could do this thing?

When she'd been accepted to this school, her heart had soared. It made her mother happy, which made Chaya happy. But that was not the only reason for her flying heart. She loved to sing — and JAPA promised to give her plenty of opportunities to do that. Long before the first day of school, Chaya had spent many long hours in her room, daydreaming about being in the choir and performing for appreciative audiences everywhere.

What she had conveniently *not* thought about was... math.

Ugh! The very word made her feel like throwing up.

Ever since she was a little kid, every subject in school had come easily to her — except math. For some reason, numbers never did what she wanted them to. No matter how hard she tried to hold on to them, they wriggled out of her grasp like a bunch of slippery eels. How she envied girls who could whiz through a math problem and come up with the right answer without even seeming to try!

For Chaya, most of the time, forget about finding the correct answer. She couldn't even understand the question!

Somehow, she'd managed to squeak by until this year.

But JAPA was a stricter school than the one she'd been in before. Mrs. Mammon, the principal, had made it very clear that she would not tolerate failing marks. In this school, it was sink or swim.

Chaya could swim beautifully through her other subjects. It was math that was going to sink her.

At the thought, she buried her face even more deeply in the crook of her already soaked elbow and sobbed her heart out in the hushed and empty room.

From where I stood near the staircase, I could hear the tramp of feet and the babble of voices as girls went down to the lobby, but I didn't follow them. Even Penny had already gone ahead. I guess she didn't see what I had seen.

What I'd seen was Chaya… hurrying down the corridor in the opposite direction from the rest of us.

I hesitated another second. Choir practice would be starting in ten minutes, and I didn't want to be late.

But my curiosity would not let me turn around and walk down the stairs like everyone else. I *had* to see where Chaya had gone! It was a mystery, and I've always loved reading mystery stories. The questions, the clues, and finally learning the secrets that let you understand everything…

So I turned away from the stairs and hurried back the way Chaya had gone. Past our math classroom, past a few other classrooms, to the very end of the hall.

The door of the last room was closed — but it had

been open before. I was sure of it. Anyway, this was the end of the hall. There was no place else to go.

Was Chaya in there? I put my ear close to the door, listening. I didn't hear voices… but I did hear something else. My eyes grew round. I hesitated some more, thinking fast.

This was none of my business. If Chaya wanted anyone to know why she was crying, she would have told her good friend Penny. But she had *not* told Penny. She'd left in a rush when the bell rang after math class, practically flying out the door to get away from everyone.

Why?

I shook my head. If Chaya had not told Penny where she was going, she certainly wouldn't want to tell anyone else. Especially me. I was the last person she'd want to confide in.

I stood on the spot, undecided. The easiest thing to do would be to turn right around and head back down the hall and down the stairs. I could pretend that I'd never seen Chaya go this way. I could make believe I'd never heard her sobbing in the empty classroom. In a few seconds I could be milling around the lobby like everyone else, waiting for music prep to start.

Instead, very slowly, I twisted the knob and pushed open the door.

Chapter 39

The Decision

I stared at Chaya. She stared at me. Her damp eyes were swollen from her tears, and pink around the edges.

"What's wrong?" I blurted.

She continued to stare at me, not answering. And could I really blame her? What reason had I ever given her for trusting me even the tiniest bit?

I could have simply turned around and walked back out of the room. That would have been the easy thing to do. Here was a girl I envied. The girl who had taken my place with Penny. The girl who was way prettier than me and whose voice was better than mine. I had no idea why she was crying, but it was none of my business. *Just go*, a little voice urged inside my head.

But I didn't want to go. Call it curiosity. Call it anything you want. Maybe I just wanted to prove to myself that jealous or not, I *was* capable of being nice. So I tried again.

"You don't have to tell me if you don't want to," I said, making sure to keep my voice gentle and non-threatening. "But maybe I can help."

Her eyes grew rounder. As if she were shocked to hear what I'd just said. And as if I were the *last* person she would ever have expected to offer to help her. Seeing her reaction made me feel kind of squirmy. Embarrassed.

Okay, more than just embarrassed. It made me feel ashamed. I'd acted pretty creepy to Chaya ever since we met, even though she'd been nothing but nice to me. Thinking of it made me get all hot and prickly inside, and I felt that *I* was about to start crying, too.

Chaya's face crumpled again. "Nobody can help me," she moaned. "I'm sunk."

"Why?"

A beat of silence. We were in a quiet room at the end of a quiet hall on a quiet floor. It felt as if the two of us were the only two people left on the planet.

"Why?" Chaya repeated. I saw her hesitate. And then she took a deep breath and decided to take the plunge.

"I'm going to fail math," she said, her face all scrunched up as if she were doing her best not to start sobbing again. "And then I'll get kicked out of the choir. And then I'll get kicked out of school." She heaved a long, shuddering sigh. "*That's* what's wrong."

My mouth dropped open. Quick as a flash, I remembered what the principal had said about keeping our grades up. Mrs. Mammon took things like that seriously. Very seriously.

I backtracked to the beginning of what she'd said. "Why do you think you're going to fail math? We only had one test so far. And a couple of quizzes."

I knew that she hadn't done well on the test because I'd seen her face when the test was returned. I was about to ask about her quiz marks when I realized that I didn't have to. Chaya was sitting here crying because she was afraid that she was failing math. *Duh.*

"It's not so hard," I said encouragingly. "Maybe you could —"

"It's hard for *me*, okay?" For the first time, Chaya's expression stopped being gloomy and started being a little angry. I'd never seen her look that way before. Usually, she wore a sort of beautiful-but-bashful smile for everyone. But she had no smiles for me right now.

I backed off, fast. "Got it. Math is hard for you. You didn't do well on the quizzes or the test, and now you're afraid you'll fail the test next week."

Chaya nodded. A sound that was halfway between a gulp and a hiccough came from her throat. "And don't tell me to ask my parents for a tutor. They — they're so proud of me for being a good student. I can't tell them that I'm failing math. I just *can't*!"

Time seemed to stop. I stared some more at Chaya, and she stared back at me. I had a decision to make, here in this deserted classroom at the end of a deserted hall. And I had to make it fast. Music prep was about to start, and I didn't want to be late.

Have you ever had two different impulses fighting inside of you? That's what was going on in my heart just then.

One impulse — and it was a strong one — was to leave this whole thing alone. To walk out of the room and forget that I'd ever seen Chaya's tear-soaked face or heard what she had to say. This whole thing was none of my business. *Just go.*

Or maybe… it actually *was* my business, in a way. In a not-so-nice way. If Chaya got kicked out of JAPA, there went the competition. No more super-stunning voice to compete with mine in choir. No more worrying about who Penny liked more. I'd be rid of my biggest headache. Free and clear. On top of the world.

But Chaya was more than just a great voice or my biggest headache. Right now, she was a girl with a problem. A problem that I could solve.

That was the second impulse that was fighting with the first one. The impulse to finally stop being mean to Chaya and do something nice for her instead.

Jealousy is like a room, Mrs. Mammon had told me. When you feel the urge to go in, she'd said, just remember one thing: *Don't go in!*

Mommy had advised me not to ever open the door of the jealousy room. But sometimes the door is open before you realize it. Without thinking, you find yourself already inside, standing right in the middle of the room. What are you supposed to do then?

I answered my own question: *You go back out and slam the door shut.*

I closed my eyes for a second, picturing myself stepping *out* of the room and shutting that wide-open door. SLAM!

I opened my eyes and smiled at Chaya, who was gaping at me as if she wondered what in the world I was doing.

"It's going to be okay," I announced.

She nodded gloomily. "Yeah, right."

"It's going to be okay," I repeated, "because I'm going to help you."

"Oh, really? How do you plan to do that?" I could tell that Chaya didn't want to even *start* hoping there was a way out of her problem.

Very slowly, as if she were a wild animal in the woods that I didn't want to scare off, I pulled a desk closer and sat down.

"It's like this," I said. "Math happens to be my thing. I'm good at it. Really good."

Her eyes grew round again.

"In fact — not boasting or anything — in my old school I *aced* my math tests. Top of the class. Kids came to me for help all the time."

For the first time, hope dawned on Chaya's face. "You actually understand the stuff we've been learning?"

I snapped my fingers. "It's a cinch."

"For you, maybe." She frowned.

"That's what I've been telling you. But I can make it easy for you, too. We can —" I paused, as I realized just how enormous this was. "We can study together, if you want."

Wow. I couldn't believe I'd just done that.

Chaya couldn't believe it either. Not at first.

But as the announcement for music prep came over the intercom and we started hustling downstairs, she began to look happier and happier. By the time we reached the lobby, she was smiling again.

"Tonight?" she asked, just before we burst into Room 8 for choir practice.

I didn't even hesitate.

"Tonight," I agreed.

Chapter 40

Pile on the Rewards!

Miss Sperling was just about to begin choir practice. She turned toward the door as Chaya and I barged in, frowning because we'd made it at the very last minute.

Then she looked again. She saw us — together. And she began to smile.

"Take your places, girls," was all she said.

We ran through the first song once, but the harmony came in late and some of us messed up the lyrics at the end. Miss Sperling told us to stop.

"Listen up," she said, planting herself in front of us and making sure to catch the eye of each and every girl in that choir. "You may think that Chanukah is a long time off, and that we have tons of time to practice. But you'd be wrong!" She glared. "The time is going to melt away before you know it. And when you stand up there on the stage to sing, you're not going to be singing just for yourselves. You're going to be doing it for this amazing school of ours! A school," she said, lowering her voice solemnly, "that is just starting out and is still a bit shaky on its legs."

"What does that mean?" someone called out.

"It means that we're going to need a lot of support to keep going. And that means having people decide to hire us to perform for them. And *that* means practice. Lots and lots of practice. So much practice that you'll be able to do these harmonies in your sleep!"

Someone in the back row closed her eyes and pretended to snore. Miss Sperling was not amused.

"If there's anyone here who does not intend to give one thousand percent to this performance, you'd better tell me about it now. And," she added grimly, "you might as well walk out that door now, too." She pointed dramatically at the door. And waited.

When no one said a peep or made a move toward the door, she put her hands on her hips and said, "Fine. I'll take that as a commitment. Now, let's take it from the top again, girls. And this time, give it everything you've got!"

We did. This time, we paid attention. We remembered all the harmonies and didn't forget a single word of the lyrics. I don't know about the others, but I pretended that I was in the hall at the actual performance, singing so that they could hear me at the back of the gigantic room.

When we were done, Miss Sperling nodded her head. We felt pretty proud of ourselves. We waited for extravagant praise.

"Not bad," was all she said. "Again!"

When it was Chaya's turn to step up and sing her solo, I listened to her along with everyone else... and suddenly realized that for the first time, I didn't feel even a little bit jealous. I couldn't believe it!

Could it be because I'd just offered to help her? I wasn't sure. All I knew was that every note she sang sent me soaring toward the sky. I was grinning with pleasure by the time she was done. With Chaya on our team, we were going to ace this thing for sure!

"Ora?" Miss Sperling said. I came down from the clouds to find her looking at me. Along with everyone else.

My cheeks burned. "Um, yes?"

"Can you step up here a minute?" She pointed to the spot next to Chaya, at the front of the choir. Right in front of Miss Sperling.

My heart lurched — and then dropped like a broken elevator. This was it. Miss Sperling had finally decided that enough was enough. I was out of the choir.

And out of the school?

In the three seconds that it took me to walk up to the front of the choir, I almost laughed — a miserable kind of laugh — when I thought about Chaya being afraid that *she'd* be kicked out for failing math. It looked like I was the one who'd be going first...

I stood where Miss Sperling had pointed and looked at her, cringing as I waited for her next words. I wished that she'd say them, whatever they were, in private instead of in front of the whole choir.

"Ora, I just had an idea," Miss Sperling said. "Chaya's solo could use an extra something. A contrast, to lend richness. I want you to sing the regular melody while she does the soprano."

I blinked. "You — you want me to sing with Chaya?"

"Exactly." She stepped back and waved her head to count down. "Three... two... one... go!"

My heart scrambled back to its right place. Chaya and I exchanged a look, surprised and a little shy.

And then we began to sing.

This was the first time the two of us had ever sung together, and I was amazed at how awesome we sounded. Who would've thought that her high, sweet notes would blend so well with my strong, lower ones?

Miss Sperling, that's who.

She and the rest of the choir seemed to hold their breaths as they listened to the way our voices rose and fell, meeting and parting, twisting gracefully around each other like flowers growing on a vine in the sun. When we sang the last note, there was complete silence in the room.

Then, spontaneously, the clapping broke out. Girls cheered. Miss Sperling looked gratified.

"Beautiful," she pronounced, smiling at me. "You've got the job, Ora. This is going to be a duet instead of a solo."

I looked quickly at Chaya to see if she minded. But she was smiling, too.

I felt a pang. If our places had been reversed, I think I would've felt bad having my moment alone in the spotlight suddenly become a shared moment for two. I guess Chaya doesn't have to worry about jealous rooms. It's only me who has to learn how to slam those doors...

But I pushed the thought out of my mind, because Miss Sperling was motioning for Chaya and me to go back to our places and for all of us to take the song from the top again. As I went where I belonged, I realized something. Something *huge*.

If Miss Sperling had just given me a part in the duet — it looked like my probation was over.

The choir aced the song. When we reached the part where the solo had been, both Chaya and I stepped forward and launched into our duet. There was no applause when we were done, but there didn't have to be.

I was already feeling about as good as a girl can feel.

Later, as we went out to the parking lot to meet our rides home, I kept one eye on Chaya as she made her way over to the carpool pickup lanes. Even though the lot was filled with loads of girls and plenty of noise, I never once lost sight of her. I saw her put her head together with Penny's, and I felt the familiar ache.

Here's the thing: I was really happy that I'd managed to rise above myself and offer Chaya help with her math. It hadn't been easy, but I knew it was the right thing to do. It made me feel like a good person — something I hadn't felt in a while.

And I was *overjoyed* about singing a duet with her in the performance. It felt like a gift from Hashem for offering that help. As if the second thing had come as a reward for the first thing. I was so grateful!

But no matter how thrilled I was, there was a part of

me that was still sad. There was an empty place inside me that missed Penny something fierce. Just seeing the two of them whispering together like that made me feel… not jealous, exactly. Mostly lonely.

I was about to stop watching them when I suddenly saw Penny break away. She began racing across the yard. Like a guided missile moving at top speed, she headed right in my direction. Just the way she'd done on the last day of camp, before I even knew her name.

"Ora!" she squealed, throwing her arms around me as I stood there in shock. "Can I come, too?"

Seeing my stunned expression, she laughed. "I *knew* it. I *knew* you were the nicest person in the world! And now you're going to help Chaya pass math. I can use some help, too. So, can I come?"

My heart was too full for words. I just nodded, eyes shining.

"Thanks! Let's talk later to figure out a time, okay?"

I finally managed to speak. "S-sure. Any time after supper is good for me."

"Great!" With another big hug, she let me go and ran back to Chaya. A second later, I saw her mother's car pull up. And a second after *that*, the doors of my van opened and it was time to board.

I don't remember much about the ride back to Brooklyn. I didn't talk much. I didn't sleep at all. I just sat there with the others, all of us in our uniforms, all of us looking pretty much the same in the dark bus.

But there was one thing that set me apart from the others that night.

I was the girl who sat smiling all the way home.

Chapter 41

Prep and Prayer

"**H**elp!" I gasped, bursting into the room and looking around wildly. "Bassi, this room is a *disaster*!"

My sister glanced up from her book, her eyes crinkled in confusion. "It's not Erev Shabbos, is it?"

"Noooo…"

"Then why do you care what the room looks like?"

"Because," I said, dumping my backpack by the door and frantically starting to pick things up from the floor at random, "my friends are coming over to study tonight. This is their first time here, and I want this place to look —" I broke off and glared at my sister, who was still holding her book and looking at me the way you'd look at a strange new animal in the zoo. "Bassi, did you hear what I just said? I need your *help*! Mommy's going to call us down to supper any minute, and my friends are coming here *right after*!"

Have I mentioned that Bassi has a very kind heart? She saw me huffing and puffing around the room like a maniac, trying to clear away scattered books and hair accessories, clean clothes and dirty ones, and she was on her feet in seconds. Without a word, she went over to her bed and began straightening the covers.

"You do your side of the room, and I'll do mine," she said. "Don't worry, Ora. This won't take long."

She was right — it didn't. With the two of us working together, the room was back in order in no time at all. Things that had been on the floor were out of sight in drawers. Books were on their shelves. Clothes were hung up in the closet or dumped in the hamper. Hair accessories were right where they belonged.

"Whew! We did it!" I stopped, suddenly a little shy. "Uh, thanks for helping, Bassi. You were great."

"My pleasure," she said. "I know you'd do the same thing for me."

Would I? Probably. But with a lot more grumbling. Not everyone is as nice as my big sister, that's for sure.

I felt bad about the way I'd yelled at Bassi, but I had a feeling she knew I hadn't meant it. I still couldn't believe that Penny was actually coming over! After nearly two weeks of silence, she would be right here in my room. Unbelievable!

Chaya would be here, too. In fact, Chaya was the reason Penny was coming. But I couldn't let myself care about that. I would be happy with what I had and stop wishing it was different. I'd made up my mind not to be jealous — SLAM! — and, with Hashem's help, I wouldn't be.

I hoped with all my heart that Hashem would help me,

because I knew how hard it was not to open that particular door…

Anyway, I told myself, what difference did it make why Penny was coming? The important thing was that she was coming. The minute she'd heard about my offer to Chaya, she'd practically begged to be invited, too.

I was flying high.

Supper was good, but I hardly tasted it. I could hardly sit still in my seat. In my excitement, I wiggled and jiggled so much that Binny said crossly, "Ora, you just shook the whole table and made my drink spill over. Quit it already!"

"Maybe you shouldn't fill your glass to the top, Binny," Mommy said mildly. She looked at me with curiosity. "Are you okay, Ora? Your cheeks are all flushed. Do you feel feverish?"

"No — I'm fine! I forgot to tell you that Penny and Chaya are coming over soon. They need me to explain the math to them. Big test next week!"

I tried to speak calmly, because I hated when members of my family exchanged The Look. The one that said, "There goes Ora — in one of her moods again."

But I guess I wasn't calm enough, because my little sister Huvi began squealing, "I want to see them when they come! Can I see them, Ora?" And Shmulie, not to be outdone, picked up on the excitement in the air and began pounding on his highchair tray with his spoon.

"What a ruckus!" Abba exclaimed, putting his hands

over his ears. But he was grinning. "You'd think the Queen of England was coming."

It's better than that, I thought happily. Who needs kings or queens when you can have a friend you thought you'd lost about to walk through your door in just… I checked the time on my watch.

"Yikes!" I yelped, leaping to my feet. "They're supposed to be here in ten minutes! Ma, can I be excused from clearing the table today?"

"That's fine," she said, with a loving look. She was happy to see me so happy. "Good luck with the math."

"Thanks!" And I was off!

Up the stairs, into my room, and straight to the mirror. I brushed my hair and then took a last look around. The room looked fine. It was ready for my friends.

I hoped that *I* was ready, too. Just to make sure, I whispered, "Hashem, please, please help me get it right tonight. Please help me not to get all jealous and cranky when I see how close Penny and Chaya are. And please let Penny remember that she likes me, too…"

"Ora!" Bassi called from below. "Your friends are here!"

I'd been so busy davening that I hadn't even heard the bell ring. I had planned to be on hand by the front door when they arrived. Bassi had agreed to stay out of the room while we studied, so she'd stayed downstairs. She was the one who let my friends in instead of me.

Willing my thudding heart to settle down, I went downstairs to meet them.

Chapter 42

Slamming Doors

It felt weird ushering Penny and Chaya into my room. Weird in a nice kind of way.

"Wow! Great room!" Penny looked around. Her eyes were sparkling. Her whole face was sparkling. "I can't believe this is the first time I'm seeing it, Ora!"

"Yeah, me, too." I was glad she liked my room, though Penny is the kind of girl who would probably have called the room great even if it was anything but. Just to make me feel good.

Chaya nodded. "Yes, it really is." She was a little shy with me. A little uncomfortable. Not that I blamed her. I felt the same way. We were like two strangers dancing with each other at a wedding. Both of us doing the same thing, but hardly knowing each other.

Well, at least I knew Penny. The two of us had clicked from the first time we met. But I didn't want to make the mistake of focusing only on her and making Chaya feel bad. Still, when Penny sat on my desk chair, I couldn't help perching at the foot of my bed nearby. Chaya pulled over the chair from Bassi's desk so that we made a triangle.

"Math first, or shmooze first?" Penny asked brightly.

"Nosh first," I announced, and jumped up to get some.

By the time I came back, my arms full of good things to eat and drink, the two of them seemed to feel perfectly at home. They were chattering away so happily that I wondered if they even noticed I'd been away…

Stop it, I told myself sternly. *You're just making yourself miserable.*

But that's the whole problem with jealousy: It makes you miserable.

I took a deep breath and imagined a wide-open door. I imagined myself grasping the doorknob. SLAM!

"Ora? Are you okay?" Penny asked. "You look strange."

"A little red in the face," Chaya added, looking concerned.

"I'm fine." I dumped the stuff I'd brought on my desk and motioned for my guests to help themselves. "Guess I took the stairs too fast or something."

To my relief, they didn't ask any more questions. Penny said something about school, and then I said something else, and pretty soon all three of us were having a conversation. I made sure to address Chaya, too. I didn't want a repeat of Penny's disappointment that time we'd been at her house on Shabbos. I didn't want her to think I was mean. I didn't want to *be* mean.

But it was hard to feel nice when, a minute later, Penny's laugh came out as a high-pitched squeal, and she said to Chaya, "Hey, did you hear that? I just sounded the way my flute did the other day. Remember?"

"When you tried to hit that high note," Chaya said. They both broke down in giggles, having a good laugh over a memory I didn't share...

SLAM!

That memory led to another one, and then another. Well, what did I expect? I hadn't been hanging around with them these past couple of weeks, and you can pile up plenty of memories in that time. *They* certainly seemed to have. Penny kept trying to explain things to me, and I tried to look interested. I was only being polite, though. I wasn't all that interested in the memories they had made together. I was interested in making *new* memories — ones that included me!

But how could we do that, if all they wanted to do was talk about stuff I knew nothing about?

I clenched my fists behind my back, trying hard not to feel left out. If I said the wrong thing now, I'd be right back where I was yesterday: on square one. But it was no use: I *did* feel left out.

So I went to the next step. I tried not to go from there to my old friend — or rather, my old enemy. Feeling jealous.

Your emotions are not in charge of you. You can control them.

That's what Mrs. Mammon had told me, the day she put me on probation in choir.

And I remembered something else. Something that my mother had told me once, when we talked about managing my moods.

"But what if I can't help it?" I remembered asking.

"What if I feel those things anyway?"

"Then pretend," Mommy had told me. Seeing my face fall, she added, "Not forever, Ora. If you practice enough, it will become natural. And then you won't have to pretend anymore."

Well, it wasn't natural yet. I *naturally* still felt jealous when the two girls I'd invited to my house kept talking about things I had no part of.

But I didn't have to let the feeling control me. **SLAM!**

"*Oy!*" Penny suddenly yelped. I was so startled that I gave a little jump and dropped the pretzel I'd been holding. "We're not being nice to Ora. Let's not talk about this stuff anymore, Chaya."

That was fine with Chaya. She nodded at Penny and then looked worriedly at me.

I took another big breath. I smiled. "So! Anyone interested in a little math action?"

Penny heaved a mournful sigh. "I guess we have to be."

"That's why we're here," Chaya added. She still looked worried, but her eyes were grateful.

I opened my math book, took out a pencil and paper — and I was in my element!

My friends hung on every word as I patiently explained the math to them. I showed them how to do the sample problems, and then had them do some themselves. When they got the answers wrong, I showed them why. Over and over we worked, until suddenly Chaya put down her pencil and stared at me, her blue eyes as big as saucers. "You know something? I think I actually understand this!" She shook her head in disbelief. "I'm actually starting to get this stuff!"

"Me, too," Penny said. "You're an amazing teacher, Ora!"

I beamed with pleasure. "And you guys are amazing students. Want to do one last problem before we call it quits?"

We ended up doing two more problems, because Penny messed up the first one. To my surprise, Chaya aced them both.

"Looks like you're not so bad at math after all," I told her.

"It's because you explained it so clearly," Chaya said, eyes shining. "You actually made me stop being afraid of it."

"Nothing to be afraid of," I said breezily.

Penny caught sight of the time. "Oh, no! My father should be here any minute. In fact..." She ran to the window. "...he may even be waiting outside right now."

They got up and scrambled for their things. Chaya couldn't stop thanking me. I waved off her thanks, but they made me feel good. I realized, to my surprise, that I cared about how Chaya would do on the math test. I cared a lot.

"You can thank me by coming back again soon," I said as I walked them to the door. I grinned at Penny, and then at Chaya. "Both of you."

Again to my surprise — I meant it.

I opened the door, and Penny looked out. "Yep, there's the car. Bye, Ora." She gave me an impulsive hug. "See you tomorrow."

"Tomorrow," I agreed, my heart lighter than it had been in ages.

"Tomorrow," Chaya said in her soft way.

And then they were gone.

I was halfway up the stairs when voices from below made me stop. I looked down. My father was escorting a man to the front door, just as I had done a minute before. I didn't know who the man was, but he looked somehow familiar.

Then my father's voice floated up to me, clear as a bell.

"Goodnight, Mr. Grossbaum. See you in shul tomorrow, I hope."

I didn't hear the answer, because I'd turned around and fled back to my room.

Mr. Grossbaum! My heart sank.

Had he come here to complain about what my brother had done?

And would this make Binny madder at me than ever?

Chapter 43

Plans for Binny

Binny was in shock.

It had been such an ordinary day. Nothing memorable. Nothing that stood out or made it different from any other day.

Until tonight.

He'd been in his room after supper, kicking a soccer ball around even though he knew his mother didn't like it very much. Kicking a ball was the only way he knew to calm himself down when he was feeling upset. And he was sure feeling that way now. Who wouldn't be, when they'd been grounded for a whole week and were missing out on *everything*?

He heard his father go out to shul for Minchah and Maariv, and after a while he heard him come back. So far, everything was normal. Just the way it was every night.

And then, in one second, everything changed.

"Binny?" His father knocked on his door and then

opened it. "Can you come downstairs for a minute?"

Binny looked at his father in surprise. When Abba had knocked on his door, he'd assumed that he was going to get a scolding for kicking the ball in his room again. But his father didn't even seem to notice the black-and-white soccer ball that Binny was trying to unobtrusively push out of sight in the well of his desk.

"Downstairs?" he repeated. "What for?"

"There's someone here to see you."

Wondering who it was, Binny followed his father out of the room and down the stairs. With each step, he grew more uneasy. He was nine years old, but he suddenly felt much younger. He felt like a little kid, walking into the unknown. A little kid who wanted his parents to protect him from... whatever was coming.

Abba led the way into the living room, where a man was sitting on the couch. The man gave Binny a half-smile when he saw him, but Binny didn't smile back. He was too busy panicking.

Mr. Grossbaum!

"Good evening, Binyamin," his elderly neighbor said formally.

"G-g-g-ood..." It took three tries before Binny managed the word "evening."

"Have a seat, Binny," his father said. He seemed as relaxed as Binny was nervous. "Mr. Grossbaum came home from shul with me because he wants to talk to you."

"T-talk? T-to me?"

"That's right."

Binny forced himself to look directly at Mr. Grossbaum. "Is it because...?" He faltered. He wasn't sure if what he'd been about to say would get him in even bigger trouble.

Mr. Grossbaum was glad to help him out. "Yes," he said with a nod. "It's about the time you climbed my fence — or tried to. I understand that you fell. Are you okay now?"

"I'm fine," Binny mumbled. His head was whirling. When his parents had grounded him for climbing the fence, he'd assumed that it was Ora who had told them about it. Had *Abba* gone and told Mr. Grossbaum?

"H-how did you find out?" he asked. "You weren't even home that day." He blushed. "At least, I didn't see your car…"

"I *was* away," Mr. Grossbaum said. "I went to my son's house for Succos. But my neighbor saw you. She told me all about it when I came home." Gravely he added, "I'm glad to see you've recovered."

"I'm sorry!" Binny blurted, cheeks flaming. "I won't ever do it again!" He'd already been grounded for a week. If Mr. Grossbaum was really mad, would his parents extend that to a month?

His neighbor settled himself more comfortably on the couch. "Tell me something, young man," he said. "Why is it so important for you to cut through my yard?"

"I cut through everyone's yards," Binny said. "That's the fastest way to get to where I'm going."

"Which is?"

"My friend Yitzi's house, around the corner. You see, he only lets the first few kids who come play basketball. If I get there late, I have to wait for *ages* to join the game." His shoulders slumped. "If ever."

"Yes." Mr. Grossbaum nodded. "That's what your sister said."

Binny stared. "My *sister*?"

"Ora, she said her name was. She explained it all to me. In fact, she seemed to disapprove of my putting up a fence in the first place."

"She *did*?"

Another nod. Mr. Grossbaum hesitated, and then, in a different kind of voice said, "Shall I tell you why I put up that fence, Binyamin? It's because of my flower beds. My wife planted them, may she rest in peace. She loved those flowers. Now that she's gone, I don't want anything to happen to them."

Binny remembered that Mr. Grossbaum's wife had passed away not so long ago. He must be very sad. No wonder he wanted to protect the flowers that his dear wife had planted.

"I'm sorry," Binny said again. Now *his* voice was different, too. "I really am. If I messed up any of the flowers, I — I didn't mean to."

"I know you didn't. And I know that having the fence there is hard for you," said Mr. Grossbaum. "So, here's what I was thinking."

Binny looked up curiously. He glanced at his father, who was sitting quietly and listening to them talk.

"If I take down the fence, will you promise to be very careful about my flower beds?"

"For sure! Absolutely!" Binny couldn't help grinning from ear to ear. Instead of being mad, Mr. Grossbaum was offering to do just what Binny wished he would do. "Thank you, Mr. Grossbaum!"

"Not so fast, Binny," his father said, speaking up for the first time. "There's more."

Binny transferred his gaze to his neighbor, who nodded. "That's right. I'm getting older, and my knees are not what they used to be. I could use some help with weeding those flowerbeds in the spring and summer. Would you like to help me?"

Binny was surprised. This was the last thing he'd expected. He looked at his father again and knew just what his father wanted him to say.

Then he realized something else. He wasn't going to say it just because Abba wanted him to. This was something *he* wanted. Something he wanted to do for his elderly neighbor who lived all alone, but who had come over and offered to take down his fence just because he cared about Binny making it over to his friend's house a little faster.

"I will help you, Mr. Grossbaum," he said, sitting up straighter. Just a few minutes earlier, he'd felt far younger than his nine years. Now he felt much older. He felt almost grown up. He was taking responsibility.

"Thank you," Mr. Grossbaum said, with the same grave courtesy as before. "If you could come by on Sunday afternoons and maybe one other day during the week, that would be a big help."

"I sure will, *bli neder*. And — and thanks again for taking down the fence!"

There wasn't much more after that. Binny and his father walked Mr. Grossbaum to the front door, where he shook hands with both of them. That made Binny feel *really* grown up. Then Binny went back to his room to think about what had just happened.

His soccer ball was lying right where he'd left it, but he didn't need to kick it anymore. He lay back on his bed, arms crossed behind his head as he gazed up at the ceiling. He thought about everything that Mr. Grossbaum had said, and about everything that *he* had said.

Suddenly, he had another thought. Ora! He had blamed her for telling on him, when she'd actually done nothing of the kind. On the contrary — according to Mr. Grossbaum, his sister had actually tried to defend him to their neighbor.

Binny remembered how meanly he'd been treating her lately because he blamed her for his grounding. He sat up in bed. There was something he had to do before he could be truly happy about the way things had turned out. It wouldn't be easy... but he was going to do it right now.

He went to the door, out of his room, and across the hall to the room his sisters shared.

Binny took a deep breath and knocked on the door.

Chapter 44

A Better Future

I heard Abba and Binny walk Mr. Grossbaum to the door. A few seconds later, I heard Binny climb up the stairs to his room. I heard the door close.

I had questions. Why had Mr. Grossbaum come to our house tonight? What kind of trouble was Binny in?

And the biggest question of all: Was my brother going to be mad at me forever?

Though none of this was my fault, I still felt responsible somehow. They say that when you save a person's life, you become responsible for them. I had not saved Binny's life — but I *had* helped bandage his cut when he fell off Mr. Grossbaum's fence. Now I felt as if it was up to me to help my brother if I could. But how could I help him if I didn't even know what was going on?

I was about to gather my courage and go knock on Binny's door, when Bassi's voice reached me from downstairs.

"Ora! Phone call!"

Wondering who it could be, I clattered down the stairs to the living room and picked up the extension there. Mommy and Bassi were in the kitchen, Huvi and Shmulie were in bed already, and I knew that Binny was in his room. Abba was nowhere in sight. I had the living room to myself. I settled on the couch and picked up the phone.

"Hello?"

"Hi, Ora."

At the sound of her voice, my skin went cold. Why was Penny calling me the minute she got home? Was she upset with me? Had I done something wrong?

"Hi!" I said, trying to sound unconcerned even though my heart was thumping like a drum. "What's up? Are you okay?"

"Everything's fine, *baruch Hashem*. I just wanted to talk to you alone. Without Chaya."

My heart drummed even more furiously. "Why?"

"Because I wanted to say… thank you."

"For the math?"

"That, too. But for much more than that." I heard Penny take a big breath. "For turning yourself completely around. For being so nice to her." Before I could say a word, she rushed on, "Remember what it was like that Shabbos when you were both at my house?"

I felt the heat rise to my cheeks. "Um, yeah…"

"Well, you were the exact opposite tonight. You were so nice! And the whole idea of offering to help Chaya with the math in the first place was super nice. So — thank you!"

I felt such a confusion of emotions that I couldn't talk. After a few seconds, Penny asked, "Do you mind that I said all that? I didn't mean to hurt your feelings or anything. Just the opposite!"

My tongue was still locked up.

"Talk to me, Ora," Penny begged.

I cleared my throat. "I don't know what to say."

"Think of something."

"Um… you're welcome?"

Penny laughed. And suddenly, I was laughing, too. It felt nice. No, more than that. It felt — amazing! Like a big gulp of air when you've been suffocating. Or a cold glass of water when you've been dying of thirst…

"I also wanted to say that I'm sorry for calling you mean that time," Penny said. "It wasn't —"

I know it's not polite to interrupt, but I did it anyway. I knew exactly what I wanted to say. What I *needed* to say.

"No," I broke in. "You don't have to say you're sorry, Penny. *I* do. Because… what you said was right. I *was* mean."

It was Penny's turn to be quiet for a few seconds. Then she asked, "Why? What did you have against Chaya? She's one of the nicest people I ever met!"

"I know," I said — and I meant it. It had never been about not liking Chaya. It was always about me and my stupid jealousy. About not wanting to be second fiddle, ever again.

Penny was still waiting for an answer. I scrambled to come up with a good one. Then I decided to just give her the truth. Deep down, she'd probably already guessed it anyway.

"I was kind of jealous, you know?" I said hesitantly. "Because you seemed to like her so much."

"But I liked *you*, too. I still do!" Penny gave a frustrated groan. "Why can't we *all* be friends?"

Penny wasn't jealous like I was. She had no idea why it had been so hard for me to let Chaya into our friendship.

But I'd let her in tonight. And it had worked out pretty well!

"You know something?" I said slowly. "That's the best idea I've heard in a long time."

A sound came through the phone, as if Penny was letting out a breath she'd been holding.

"So… tomorrow, at school?" she asked. "It's going to be different?"

"Different how?"

"You, and me, and Chaya. No more problems. Right?"

I sat up straighter. "No more problems," I promised. I would just keep on slamming the doors that led to those jealousy rooms. Until one day, I hoped, the rooms would just disappear.

"Great!" Penny sounded as glad as I felt. I heard someone say something at her end, and then she said, "Sorry, my sister needs the phone. Talk to you at school tomorrow!"

"Tomorrow," I echoed happily.

It was the most beautiful word in the world.

I hung up the phone and climbed the stairs, feeling as if I were in a dream. Parts of the past couple of weeks had been a nightmare, but it was all different now. If this was a dream, I didn't want to wake up!

Hardly had I returned to my room, when there came

a knock on the door. I got up and opened it. Standing in the doorway, looking sheepish, was Binny.

I was glad to see him, but I was also a little wary. The past few times I'd said anything to my brother, he'd practically bitten my head off. But I did want a chance to explain why he had no reason to be mad at me. *And* to find out why Mr. Grossbaum had been to our house.

I peered at him, trying to read his mood. "Binny!"

He nodded. "Can I come in for a second?"

I held the door open wider and backed away. "Sure."

When we were both standing in the middle of the room, Binny shuffled his feet for a bit while I waited. Then he burst out, "Look, I was wrong. You didn't tell Mommy and Abba about the whole fence thing. So, I'm sorry."

"I *told* you I didn't tell them." Or I'd tried to, anyway.

"Yeah, well…" At my accusing words, Binny started to look as if he wished he were someplace else. This wasn't the way I wanted this scene to go.

"Okay, you're forgiven," I said hastily. "But why was Mr. Grossbaum here? That *was* him just now, right?"

My brother nodded. Suddenly, his eyes were shining. "It sure was! And you'll never believe what he said…"

I listened, spellbound, to the story of Binny's meeting with our neighbor.

"So the fence is coming down, and you're going to help him weed his flowerbeds?"

"Yes! Isn't that the coolest thing ever?"

I nodded. I was glowing, too. "I think *Mr. Grossbaum* is the coolest ever!"

I went to bed soon afterward. I felt as if the day had

been too full to go on a minute longer. Propped up against my pillows, I thought about everything that had happened.

When I'd woken up that morning, I was still a girl who'd been missing Penny for a long time. And who'd been feeling jealous of Chaya for just as long. I never dreamed that both of them would be at my house tonight. Or that we'd all be friends at last!

I thought about my brother, too. When Binny woke up this morning, he had no clue that Mr. Grossbaum would come over that evening to say that he was going to tear down the fence on his property and let Binny come through whenever he liked. Or that Binny would agree to help him with his flowers. Such a nice, neighborly thing to do!

I guess you can never tell what the day will bring.

Smiling, I thumped my pillow and settled down for sleep. After what had happened today — I just couldn't wait to see what tomorrow would be like!

Chapter 45

Work... or Fun?

"**Y**ou're looking happy this morning," Mommy said, in between stirring the scrambled eggs, pouring Huvi's hot cocoa, and making sure Shmulie didn't fall out of his highchair.

I remembered the last time my mother had said the same thing to me. It had been a day that had started out happy but ended up being the exact opposite. I hoped with all my heart that today would turn out very differently.

"I *am* happy," I said, taking my seat at the table. "I'm starving, too. Are there enough eggs for me?"

"More than enough. So, what's making you so happy, Ora?"

This wasn't exactly the time or the place for a heart-to-heart talk, but I wanted to answer my mother's question honestly. After all, she's had to put up with my bad moods for twelve years. The least I could do was share the good times with her, too.

"I worked things out with my friends," I said. "At least, I hope so."

"You hope so?"

"I hope I can keep it up." I made a face.

Mommy paused with the spatula in the air to give me a long look. "What do you mean?" she asked.

"You know — not being jealous. Stuff like that."

"You're jealous?" Huvi asked. She'd been sitting with her nose an inch away from the cereal box, trying to find letters of the alphabet that she recognized. Trust my little sister to prick up her ears at the wrong moment!

"Uh, not anymore," I told her. I prayed that my words would come true.

"Oh! That's good, right?"

I gave her a big smile. "The best."

My mother was smiling, too. "It *is* the best, Ora. And I'm sure you can keep it up. Try never to let negative feelings creep up on you unawares. Always be prepared for a sneak attack. Know what I mean?"

I pictured my moods like wild animals, creeping through the jungle where I couldn't see them. Without any warning — they pounced! Before I knew it, I was down in the dumps, or seething with envy, or anger, or a million other things that I didn't want to feel. I'd have to keep my eyes open if I didn't want that to happen to me anymore.

I nodded. I knew exactly what Mommy meant.

Then the toast popped out of the toaster, and Binny came into the kitchen, followed by Bassi. Conversation over... except for a last, secret smile that Mommy and I shared before she started dishing out the eggs and toast.

✿ ✿ ✿

The next few weeks sped by like racing cars zooming along an empty highway. It was hard to catch my breath!

Imagine having a full load of classes and schoolwork. And then imagine, on top of *that*, rehearsing for a super-important performance. Our first performance of the year, on Chanukah, was super important *because* it was the first. It would be our introduction to the whole Jewish community. Our reputation was riding on it!

We were a terrific Bais Yaakov *plus* a school for the performing arts. There were lots of people who had scoffed at the idea when Mrs. Mammon and her supporters first began talking about it. I knew that because Mrs. Mammon told us so at one of our assemblies.

"People said that it would never work," she said to the rows and rows of students filling the auditorium. "Some of them are *still* saying it." She gazed out at us and started to smile. "Well, we have something to prove, girls. We have to prove that what we're trying to do here *can* work. And that it *is* working!"

When the cheers died down, she continued talking.

To do that, she explained, we'd have to use every drop of our energy to be the best students we could be, and the best performers we could be. That meant keeping up our grades, of course. And it meant tons of practice. And I mean *tons*.

Miss Sperling made us rehearse our harmonies until we knew them cold, and then rehearse them again. I knew from Penny that the band — or orchestra, as Mrs. Judowitz likes to call it — was doing the same thing.

"We have to make sure that every note is perfect," Penny told me. "*Perfectly* played, and *perfectly* on time. Let me tell you, that takes work!"

I nodded sympathetically. Chaya nodded, too. Like me, she knew how much work we were putting into our choir. And sometimes, when the three of us were down in our favorite spot in the basement before music prep, Gali would join us and describe how hard the dance group was working.

"We practice so much that I get charley horse on top of my charley horse!" she declared once, with a comical moan that made us laugh.

It's a funny thing, though. We called it "work," but it didn't feel like work at all! I guess what they say is true: If you love to do something, it stops being work and becomes fun.

Of course, we spent plenty of time complaining anyway. Complaining about how busy we were, about all the homework, and the tests, and the non-stop rehearsals.

But the truth? I was having the time of my life!

Chapter 46
The Pact

"I can't believe we're having our dress rehearsal today," Penny said in an awed voice, one cold December afternoon. Our rides home would be picking us up late today because this rehearsal would be an extra-long one.

It was Thursday, the second day of Chanukah. We normally would be going home early instead of late, but we really needed this rehearsal. Our big performance was slated to take place in just three days, on Sunday afternoon.

"I know," I said, sitting on the floor between her and Chaya. "Unreal."

"It feels like school just started yesterday," Chaya said, shaking her head in disbelief.

Before I go on, let me tell you something about Chaya. Or rather, about me and Chaya.

Even though I'd promised myself — and promised

Penny — not to be jealous of Chaya anymore, it wasn't so easy at first. Every time I saw her with Penny, the feeling would come crawling back like a wild beast in the jungle, creeping through the foliage, ready to attack.

No matter how many times I slammed the door to the jealousy room, it always seemed to open up a crack. It was like a refrigerator door whose magnet is broken. You can slam it as hard as you like — but that door will always bounce open again. It was discouraging.

And then, during choir practice one day, Chaya and I stood up to sing our duet as usual. We always sounded fine together, but that day was something special.

Our voices rose into the air like two birds soaring in graceful circles around each other. They dipped and danced until they began to sound like one voice. Two parts that blended perfectly and together created something beautiful.

It's hard to explain how I felt, hearing the music that we made. All I can say is that when our duet was done, I spontaneously turned to look at Chaya — just as she turned to look at me. Our eyes met. We both smiled.

And, just like that, I realized something.

I *liked* her.

I was not just tolerating her for the sake of keeping Penny's friendship. I wanted to be Chaya's friend, too. And I was so glad that she wanted to be mine!

I was also glad that my coaching was helping her with her math. Her mark on our next test was very different from the first.

After that, things became a lot easier. I stopped keeping track of who Penny called more or who she seemed to like better. As I'd promised her on the night we studied math together, we were *all* going to be friends. End of story.

But really, the story was just beginning.

I sat between the two of them now, in the chilly basement, with the commotion of dozens of girls milling in the lobby above our heads and the big dress rehearsal just a few minutes away. On that miserable night when I'd felt as if everything was going wrong with my life, Mommy had told me that after I learned how to deal with my jealousy, I'd have to learn how to share.

And that's just what I'd been doing. I was sharing Penny's friendship with Chaya. I was sharing the spotlight in choir with Chaya, too.

And you know what? I was as happy as I ever remembered being.

I was grateful to be a student at this amazing school. I was grateful for my friends. I wanted to be the kind of person who *deserved* such a school and such friends. I wanted to do something special, to make me feel that I deserved all that happiness.

"Remember what Mrs. Mammon told us?" I said suddenly. "Back at our first assembly? About how people think of performers as 'stars' that crave attention and praise… but that we should be different. She said that we should be like *real* stars — the ones that shower light on the world. Remember?"

On either side of me, Chaya and Penny nodded. They remembered.

I remembered other things too. Less pleasant things.

I remembered how much I'd enjoyed the admiration in

my former classmates' eyes when they visited me on Succos to hear all about JAPA. How I'd strutted around like a peacock after that visit, so proud of myself. Proud that those girls admired me just because Hashem happened to give me the gift of a good voice.

I also remembered, with burning cheeks, how smug I'd been to my sister Bassi when practicing my scales for choir. How I acted as if I were somehow superior to her, just because I could sing.

And I thought of Shayna Korman and her "We're sooo special song." How it made me feel puffed up and disgusted at the same time. *Not* a pleasant feeling.

"So, here's what I was thinking," I said, shaking off the memories. "Let's make a pact."

"A pact?" Chaya asked.

I nodded. "An agreement between the three of us. Let's agree never to become stuck-up or show-offy, just because we have a talent and a chance to use it. Let's promise to always be the *right* kind of stars!"

"*Yes!*"

"Great idea!"

My friends were all for it. I stuck out my hand. Penny put hers on top of it. Then Chaya put hers on top of Penny's.

"A pact!" I declared. "To —"

"Wait!" cried a voice behind us. The door to the janitor's closet flew open, and out tumbled Gali. She was pink-cheeked and breathless from practicing her dance steps in there. "I heard what you said. Can I join the pact, too? Please?"

We all stared at her in surprise. Then Penny and Chaya turned their heads and looked at me. After all, this was my idea.

I felt a little pang. Part of me wanted to keep this private, just between the three of us.

Then I remembered how I'd tried to be exclusive with Penny, and how well *that* had turned out. Gali was sweet and funny, and she seemed to feel just the way we did about things.

Maybe it wasn't enough just to not be jealous of people. Maybe I had to stretch in other ways, too. Learn to let people in.

I had started the year hoping to find a best friend. And now I had two of them.

Maybe even... three?

Gali was gazing at me earnestly, as if her whole life was in my hands. Her long ponytail hung down her shoulder and her hands were clasped with hope.

"So, can I?" she asked.

I gave her a big smile. "Why not?"

Gali whooped with joy. Then she ran over and put her hand on top of ours. And we made our pact.

"Everybody is to report to the auditorium for the dress rehearsal," droned the school secretary's voice over the intercom. Somehow, Mrs. Reingold managed to make even the most thrilling event sound matter-of-fact.

Our eyes lit up with excitement. All the weeks of practice had been leading up to this. Our first full dress rehearsal, with costumes and props and lighting just the way they would be on the big day.

"Let's go!" I cried. We scrambled to our feet.

With my friends right behind me, I led the way upstairs.

Chapter 47

The Performance

Bassi put on her coat and followed her mother out to the car. This was the big day! The day that Ora had been waiting for, and practicing for, practically since the first day of school.

"Hurry," her mother urged. "We don't want to be late."

It was a long drive to Valley Stream. Bassi was so excited for her sister that she could hardly sit still. "Are we there yet?" she kept asking, like a little kid and not a high-school girl at all.

The third time she asked, her mother said, "Almost."

And then — they were there. The parking lot was already half-full of cars, and Bassi could see plenty of others lining up to get in. A steady stream of women and girls were making their way into the building. The lot would soon be filled, and people would have to start parking in the streets. The wind was strong but not too cold as Bassi and her mother stepped out of the car. More like October than December.

This was the first time Bassi had seen Ora's school. She liked the shrubs that lined the front of the building, and the colorful winter flowers on either side of the glass doors. She read the words:

BAIS YAAKOV OF VALLEY STREAM

And underneath:

Jewish School for the Performing Arts

Bassi's face split into a huge smile. This building, this school, was a dream come true for Ora. And Bassi couldn't be happier for her!

Inside, the auditorium was awash in the noise of a hundred voices, all talking at once, and the rustle of coats being draped over the backs of chairs. From behind the curtain on the stage, someone tapped a microphone and said, "Testing, one, two, three." Bassi tried to catch a glimpse of her sister, but all the performers were behind the curtain, waiting for the signal to start the show.

While she waited, Bassi thought again about what had happened at home, just before Ora left the house that morning. The girls had to be at their school early for a last dress rehearsal before the performance, and Ora was in a hurry.

Bassi had tried to help her get ready. She found her missing shoe, helped do her hair, and even prepared a bag of snacks to take along because Ora was too excited to each much breakfast.

At the front door, just before Ora had run out to catch her ride, she suddenly stopped walking, turned around, and threw her arms around her sister.

Bassi had hugged her back, surprised. "What was that for?" she asked.

"For being the best sister in the universe!" To Bassi's astonishment, Ora's eyes were shiny with tears. "I'm sorry I sometimes act like a creep…"

"Don't worry about it," Bassi said quickly. "It's fine. You're a great sister, too. Now, go!"

With a wavery smile, Ora had run out the door.

The memory of that hug, and those words, had been keeping Bassi warm ever since.

A few minutes after she and her mother took their seats, a woman appeared on the stage. She looked solemn but lit up at the same time, as if there were a lantern burning inside her that shone through her eyes.

"That's Mrs. Mammon, the principal," Mommy whispered.

When the audience had settled down, the principal welcomed them to the school's very first performance.

"Most of you," she said, "are mothers, grandmothers, and sisters of our students. Some of you are honored guests from this city and other places. We're so happy to see all of you here. Thank you for taking the trouble to come."

She spoke a little about the school's mission. About teaching the girls to use their talents *l'sheim Shamayim*. How the proceeds from their performances would help their school, and other *tzedakahs* as well. When she said how proud she was of her girls, everybody clapped. Some of the younger girls in the audience cheered for their sisters.

"And now," Mrs. Mammon said, "without further ado — I'd like to present our very own JAPA girls, and their Chanukah extravaganza!"

The auditorium echoed with wild applause as the

curtain opened.

Bassi gasped — and so did plenty of other people sitting around her. The scenery on the stage was a winter wonderland: a nightscape of rolling fields of snow, glowing bluish in the moonlight. Fir trees were outlined on the horizon, sharp and black. There was a sound of the wind blowing through the trees. It was all so realistic that Bassi almost wanted to put her coat back on.

And then the performers came onstage.

Ora had told her that the show would not have different acts by the choir, dance group, and orchestra. Instead, they would all be performing together.

"I can't explain it," Ora had said. "You'll have to see what I mean."

As the show commenced, Bassi saw. The orchestra played background music while the girls danced or the choir sang. Each act ran seamlessly into the next one. In fact, the whole thing was like one big dance, with every performer in the right place at the right time, doing her part smoothly and gracefully along with the others.

Bassi waited with bated breath for her sister's solo. Or rather, her duet. She had met Chaya a few times when she and Penny came over on Shabbos afternoons. Chaya didn't talk much but she looked sweet. Remembering Ora's last year at her old school, Bassi was happy that her sister had found some real friends at last. Friends who brought out the best in her.

There she was! The spotlight swung over to Ora, who was standing in front of the choir alongside Chaya. The light made their costumes glisten as if there were diamonds sewn on them. There was a bar of music emanating from the orchestra, and the two girls lifted their voices and began to sing.

Their mingled voices rose into the air and filled the auditorium. The audience was dead silent as they listened raptly to each pure note. When the duet was over, you could almost hear them letting out the breaths they'd been holding. Mrs. Mammon had asked them not to clap in the middle of the performance, but Bassi could tell that they wanted to.

There were musical solos, too. At one point a flute piped up, each note pinging on the still air like a drop of water falling into a pond. That must be Penny, Bassi thought. She was good!

They were all good.

No, that wasn't right. They were all *fantastic*!

This was far more than the usual school performance. Every single girl in this school had been hand-picked for her outstanding talent. They had practiced endlessly until every note, every step, every move, was perfect.

She tried to pick out Ora's other friend, Gali, in the dance group. Gali lived in a different neighborhood and had only been to their house once so far. The dances were breathtaking, and Bassi loved the way they flowed together with the songs and the instrumental music.

The three parts of the performance — choir, dance, and orchestra — were like three rivers mingling with one another until they finally met in a smashing finale. The last chords crashed into the air. The dancers stopped moving and the choir's voices faded away. The girls stood frozen against the frozen landscape.

And the audience erupted!

The applause was deafening. Cheers and whistles punctuated the energetic clapping. Bassi clapped so hard that her hands hurt. In the next seat, her mother was doing the same. She wanted to say something to Mommy, but the noise was too loud to hear herself think, let alone talk. They smiled and high-fived each other instead.

Slowly, the curtain closed on the performing girls and the snowy landscape. The clapping lessened. Mrs. Mammon came out in front of the curtain and motioned for quiet. After a long few minutes, she got it.

"That was really something. Wasn't it?"

The answer came in the form of more whooping and clapping. The noise level was astounding. Mrs. Mammon's smile was enormous.

"Ladies," she cried, waving an arm. "I give you... our performers!"

The curtain opened again, to reveal the same winter scenery with the JAPA girls arrayed in front of it in artistic knots. Mrs. Mammon introduced each and every girl by name: the members of the orchestra, the choir, and the dance group. There was wild clapping and cheering for each performer. When Ora's name was called, Bassi waved frantically, hoping that her sister could see her.

Eventually, the clapping and cheering died down. The curtain was about to close again for the final time... when something strange happened.

A woman in the audience stood up. She walked up the aisle to the steps at the side of the stage. And then, as the entire audience along with the performers and Mrs. Mammon stared at her incredulously — she walked right onto the stage!

Chapter 48
Only the Beginning

I stared at the newcomer. The woman was tall, and her high-heeled shoes made her even taller. She was wearing an elegant navy suit and a perfectly combed *sheitel*. She walked right up to Mrs. Mammon, who was standing at the side of the stage with the microphone in her hand. Our principal looked thunderstruck, too.

The woman whispered a few words to Mrs. Mammon, whose eyes opened wide. Then our principal gave a big smile and handed her the microphone.

"My name," the woman told the audience, which was burning up with curiosity, "is Mrs. Benstein. I live in London."

As a murmur began to ripple through the audience, she added with a smile, "Yes, that's right. As in London, *England*."

Now the murmur became a swell of sound. Mrs. Benstein held up one elegant hand to ask for quiet. "I don't want to keep you. But when I saw this outstanding performance, I couldn't help myself. I just *had* to speak."

The murmuring died down. You could have heard a pin drop in the auditorium. My fellow choir members were just as quiet as the audience in the big auditorium. What did this woman from London want to tell us?

"I came to New York for Chanukah to be with my married children and grandchildren," Mrs. Benstein said. "Having heard about this new school, I decided to ask if I could come to the performance. And I am so glad that I did!"

She looked over the audience, and then half-turned to smile at us onstage.

"You were amazing, girls," she said. "So amazing, that I've made a decision. I am the head of a big *tzedakah* organization in London. We are planning a gala event for our women supporters later this year. And now I know exactly who I want to come and provide the entertainment for it!"

There was a split second of absolute silence. Then we went crazy! As the audience began applauding and hooting, we forgot that we were supposed to stand still until the curtain closed. We forgot everything. We started screaming and jumping up and down and hugging each other. Pandemonium!

The first person I hugged was Chaya, who was standing right next to me. Then I hugged the other members of the choir, and even Miss Sperling, whose cheeks were so red with excitement that she seemed about to explode. After that, we all ran across the stage to hug our special friends. I threw my arms around Penny. And then Gali was grabbing me and I hugged her, too.

The decibel level was through the roof! It was a long time before we realized that Mrs. Mammon had motioned for someone to close the curtain. Out of sight of the audience, we had a million questions about Mrs. Benstein's announcement. Was it true? Would we really be flying to London?

"It's true," Mrs. Mammon said, when we had settled down enough to hear her speak. "The dinner is scheduled for May." She beamed at us, her face radiant. "Girls," she cried, "get ready for an awesome year! This is only the beginning. We are going places!"

She didn't get any further, because we didn't give her a chance. The girls in the orchestra ran to get their instruments and struck up a lively tune, and the rest of us took each other's hands and began dancing in a huge circle around the principal. At some point, Miss Sperling and the other two instructors were gathered into the middle of the circle, too. We danced until we were breathless — and then we danced some more!

After a while, the big circle broke up into smaller ones. The music stopped because the orchestra girls also wanted to dance. We started singing instead. I saw Mrs. Mammon take Shayna Korman's hands and start dancing with her.

It was nice seeing Shayna, who usually acted so superior, without the usual smirk on her face. I only hoped it would last.

Then Mrs. Mammon let Shayna go back to her friends — and took *my* hand instead!

My head spun even more than the rest of me as the principal and I circled around together. It was too noisy to talk, but she gave me a smile that said all the things I wanted to hear. Things like, "You've proved yourself, Ora. You're a team player. You're a valued member of the choir — and of our school!"

You can bet that I smiled back for all I was worth.

When Mrs. Mammon moved on, I found my friends. Twirling around with Penny and Chaya and Gali, I caught glimpses of all the other circles whirling around beside us on the stage. It was like a giant kaleidoscope, turning into a different picture each second. The faces kept changing, but they were all my classmates and my schoolmates and my fellow performers. I knew most of them by now, and those I didn't know yet I would know soon. I was a part of them, and they were a part of me.

Penny was holding on to my right hand. I saw her pink cheeks, sparkling eyes, and coppery curls. On my other side was Chaya, with her stunning features and sweet, shy smile. Holding Chaya's other hand was Gali's eager face and long, floppy ponytail.

We danced together, celebrating this amazing day and looking forward to an even more amazing tomorrow. My heart swelled until it was so big that it felt like it would explode right out of my chest. I couldn't have felt more special if I'd tried!

Tugging hard with both of my hands, I made our circle move even faster... and then a bit faster than that. Everything else became a blur as my friends whirled right along with me.

We weren't doing any particular steps. We were just flying — together. They were a part of me, and I was a part of them.

The Starlight Sisters!

THE END